ANOTHER PLACE

ANOTHER PLACE

A science fiction anthology in aid of the Alf Dubs Children's Fund

Peter Sutton
Harry Manners
Richard Bendall
M M Lewis
Gary Budgen
Mike Evis
W. Freedreamer Tinkanesh
Jule Owen
MJ Rodda
Nathan J. Bezzina

For all those seeking sanctuary

CONTENTS

ABOUT THE CHARITY

Lord Alfred Dubs arrived in Britain in 1939 as a six-year-old refugee, one of thousands of Jewish children who arrived in Britain on the Kindertransport. As an adult, he has campaigned tirelessly for refugees.

The Alf Dubs Children's Fund aims to help child refugees find safe and legal routes to sanctuary and to ensure that the children's basic needs are met while their cases progress, as well as supporting them during the first stages of their lives in Britain.

We decided to put together an anthology to raise money for refugees in 2017, after the Dubs Amendment was dropped in parliament. The amendment sought to bind the government to relocate and support 3000 unaccompanied child refugees.

As of publication date, only two hundred children have been brought to Britain under the Amendment and many more, who are eligible to settle in the UK, remain stranded in refugee camps or on city streets.

Originally there was only meant to be one book, but we had such a great response from writers wanting to get involved that it quickly expanded into two: Voices along the Road collects flash fiction and poetry, and Another Place is a collection of science fiction short stories.

All of the stories and poems you'll read in the anthologies have been donated, and all of the authors, poets and editors involved have waived a fee for their work.

The book is not officially endorsed or produced by Citizens UK and Safe Passage, or The Alf Dubs Children's Fund, but all profits will be donated to the fund.

You can find out more about the Alf Dubs Fund at: http://safepassage.org.uk/what-we-do/alf-dubs-fund/

WHEN THE LAMPS GO OUT

by Peter Sutton

There's a bloated decomposing cat, its head squashed against the road, its body burst. Two seagulls argue raucously over its guts. The sun stuns the plants on the roadside verge as I watch it all through polarised glass/s and click a picture when everything is juxtaposed how I like it. The road is empty, it's been two hours forty three minutes since the last vehicle went past; an old car circa turn of the century. I have no talent for spotting cars, I have no idea of the make and model. Mosi would know I think. They didn't stop, or even acknowledge I existed. A double blink snaps a pic of the two seagulls with a stringy piece of gut linking them from beak to beak like lovers sharing spaghetti. There is a vast rumbling in the distance, felt more than heard. Fracking in the hills again. I wonder where Mosi is, I glance back at the picnic area and see no-one, I switch to IR and zoom and still nothing. He is not there anymore.

I met Mosi a month ago at a Valvepunk convention, dressed as a WW2 boffin, playing with some sort of pre-digital computer. We hit it off, spent the second night of the convention in my bedroom (and missed the costume party) and have been together ever since.

It was his idea to come to do the 'old countries' tour. You know, those places that had been big players about a century ago but have been left behind in the quantum age. It had all gone wrong for us in France. You understand those countries are mired in corruption but it's still a shock to be ripped off by proper gendarmes, they took almost everything. I was left with an old pair of glass/s and a pre-war tablet I keep for sentimental reasons that I can't even power on. Fuckers. We made it across the border into Iberia though. Should be better here, less bullshit. Then the bike crashed, some fucking virus took it out. I wonder if it was downloaded by the gendarmes when they ran our data, probably was deliberate, shitty thing couldn't even disable us near civilisation.

Mosi went into meltdown, we shouted at each other for over an hour. That's when I walked away. Got as far as this old road and had to stop as I couldn't see through the tears. Then I spotted the cat. Now I can't see Mosi and am a little scared. Your hear stories about bandits, the Basque state police keep most of them at bay but the hills are hard to patrol efficiently. I decide to return to the picnic area. The road is relatively safe I hope.

I walk back to the bike, which is still totally frizzed.

"Mosi!" I shout "Where are you? Hello?!" I am exhausted, wrung out from the emotions and from days in the saddle. There has been limited patchy reception since we got off the liner from Norway. Now there was no reception at all, these people still used radio technology. Mosi hadn't wanted to hire a phone. 'I don't see the point, what would we use it for?' was his attitude. Where the fuck is he? I'm starting to worry.

I walk around the picnic area and come to the conclusion that he's definitely fucked off and left me. Charming. What a knight in shining armour. Mind you I did walk off in a huff, but always within sight of this place. OK so he didn't pass me and he can't have walked uphill through the scrubby bushes so he must have headed south. I shrug my backpack on and start walking. I look back once, to see the bike, when I'm a few hundred metres down the road. It looks forlorn. I hope it isn't stolen, although no-one can ride it off in the condition it's in.

An hour or so later I see Mosi in the distance wandering around a ghost town. I tramp on over.

"Why d'you run off?" I ask him after we make up.

"Looking for reception or a town or anything."

"Not much here is there?" I ask

"Not really, this town has been empty for decades, maybe even since the war."

"Wow really?"

I take a closer look but the crappy houses don't look up too much.

"Hard to believe anyone used to live here, in these conditions."

"Looks like they were on the grid, should be able to follow the line of pylons to a power station or bigger town."

"Look, Mosi I'm sorry, I thought it'd be cool to come to the old world and tour around but it's clear we underestimated the hassle it would be. We'd have been better off staying in Africa or going on holiday to Brazil. I'm tired and cranky and I'm thinking of quitting... Going home."

He looks at me with understanding and relief.

"Thank God for that, I thought it was just me. Come on let's find the nearest town and organise getting home."

"What about the bike?" I ask tiredly. "Can we just leave it?"

"It's probably already gone, taken by bandits for spare

11

parts." He doesn't look upset by this.

We find a well and Mosi fills our bottles, the filters slurping at the water as if they were as thirsty as us. After a minute they beep and turn green. This water is safe. We don't have much to eat, just some trail rations. I'm not even sure how far over the border we are, never mind how far the next city is. That's the thing about technology, it's great whilst you have it but as soon as you lose signal, or battery you'd be better off with an old-fashioned paper map. The satnav is on the bike, and fried, the tablet I have is almost useless (I can spark it up if I find an induction charger) and the glass/s are only on their inbuilt memory since we have no connection out here.

"There's the remains of an old road over there." Mosi says pointing. "Let's follow it and find out where it goes. I think there was a big town on the coast a bit south from the French border?"

Having no better plan I agree with a grunt.

Mosi starts talking about the bikes he'd read about from the middle of last century, not a single computer on them. I can't wrap my head around the concept. How did they know where they were? The exact speed they were doing? The road topography? The rules of the road? Mosi says that in those days they didn't know any of those things and it didn't matter. Like I said I can't wrap my head around the concept.

We've been walking for about two hours when we catch a glimpse of the sea and a large town/small city. All very old world. I wonder if we can finally get some reception. If these people have even heard of satellites. If we can have a nice shower. It was hot as hell out here.

When a black and white bird flaps up off the road in front of us and Mosi stumbles and falls I half laugh; when he doesn't immediately spring up I bend close to him.

"Are you alright?" I ask before I spot the blood.

Just to my left there is a small explosion of dust and suddenly my brain catches up and I realise that Mosi has been shot and the shooter is now trying to shoot me. I run crazily crouched and in a zig zag pattern over to the ditch at the side of the road and dive down into it. The earth jumps up to give me a giant slap. My ears are now ringing and I am panting like a dog. Apart from the noises I am making and the sound of crickets there is silence. I realise I am saying 'shit' over and over again until it has become a meaningless sound and by a huge effort of will stop myself. I am trembling and covered in sweat. I have to have a look, to see if Mosi is dead but if I look over the top they will shoot me in the head. I remember that I can use the record function of my glass/s with the manual button and then take a look on playback. Cautiously I pop my hand, holding the glass/s above the level of the ditch and press record and do what I hope is a smooth sweep.

On playback it doesn't look good. Mosi is motionless and there is a visible pool of blood next to him. I can't see the shooter. I wonder if they are alone, waiting for me to make a break for it. What if they aren't alone and their accomplices are on their way right now to where I am hiding. How far can I get before becoming exposed? My rucksack is still on my back luckily but I have lost access to everything in Mosi's, including the gun we had bought in France. That seems like a long time ago now, we had joked that if we were attacked by bandits we probably wouldn't be able to shoot them anyway, as this gun doesn't have assisted sights. Couldn't get one on the liner though, so we agreed to make do.

I try to think but my sheer bloody terror is making it

difficult. Where to go? I hear a faint rumble which is slowly getting louder. A car! I am either saved or screwed. How am I going to get their attention if I don't stand? Actually won't they see Mosi and slow down, if not stop? I wait until it gets closer and then do a couple of quick head bobs over the top. I then scuffle my way down the ditch a little hoping it'll take the shooter some time to draw a bead.

The car approaches, slows and I leap out and run towards it. A shot explodes the ground just behind me. Then I am at the car. As I catch the door handle, and try to yank it open, the passenger side window shatters, blowing glass all over the shocked looking man in the driver's seat. He puts his foot down and the car speeds off, pulling the handle out of my hand and nearly snapping some fingers as it does so. The next shot grazes my leg as I stand stupidly looking at the rapidly receding car. It spurs me to make a run for the ditch again. As I leapfrog over the bank, the dirt nearby spurts up as a bullet passes within inches of where my head is. I take a look at the leg, the shot has gone through the muscle shallowly but it is bleeding freely. I take off my t-shirt, rip a strip off it and tie it as tight as I can around the wound.

"Fuck, fuck, fuckity fuck."

I hunker down as far as I can in the ditch and start to squirm towards the town. It's all gone quiet again. I stop and listen. It suddenly occurs to me that the shooter may not be a hill bandit, he may be a member of the town I am currently crawling to. I've heard of some towns that keep all strangers out, with force. Perhaps this is one of them. I wish Mosi was OK. He'd know what to do.

Thinking of Mosi I try again to see if he's OK. His head is turned towards the ditch, his lips are moving. I run the lip-synch app on the glass/s "help me… please…

help me" he is saying.

I find a stick, wrap my raggedy t-shirt round it and wave it over the top of the ditch.

"Hello?" I shout, my mouth dry, breath rasping. I wipe the sweat out of my eyes. There is no answer. This is, of course, a bad sign.

I tie the glass/s to the stick and press record, hold them up as high as I can without exposing myself and do a sweep. I pull up the slomo app and zoom in as much as possible. There, a few hundred metres away, a post mounted sentry bot.

It'll have an IR camera, a mobility sensor, may be remotely controlled but is more likely to just be all algorithm. It means I can't reason with the shooter.

"Mosi!"

"MOSI!"

"...ungh ...whaaaat?"

"IT'S A SENTRY BOT."

"..."

"What?"

"Mosi?"

"MOSI!"

I risk a look, Mosi has his eyes closed. He looks out of it. He is lying in a spreading pool of blood. OK. OK. It's up to me then. Bastard. Always leaving things to me. I wipe away my angry tears and see what I have in my pockets. The lighter. I have the lighter in my pocket. We'd brought it with us thinking we'd be able to stop and camp and have campfires. I hope the bot is an auto, I hope it'll go for the biggest heat signature; I hope I can carry Mosi.

The T-shirt I wrap around the log burns nicely, even though there are a couple of damp patches. I prop it up and move off. The second shot makes the stick fall over into the ditch. I drop to the ground and stop moving. I can see the bot slowly pan its sights across the road. Seems it was programmed on IR and movement, not sure if I'm about to get shot, maybe because I'm prone I'm being flagged as no danger? I am about five foot from Mosi, he doesn't look good, his skin has gone greyish and I can't tell if he's breathing. If he is it's very shallowly.

"Think, for fucks sake, think!"

It has a motion sensor so I'll have to move VERY slowly and only when the barrel of its gun is pointing away. I start to move, slowly, slowly. I hear it above the crickets, a machine whirr, a servo working. I stop moving. I wait, watch it sweep around, at its furthest point I move again. Slowly, painstakingly, keeping my eye on it, playing a game of freeze. It feels like hours pass as the sun burns my back as I move across the road like I'm swimming through molasses. That sunburn is going to sting later. As long as there is a later. I should have taken the time to grab a spare t-shirt.

When my hand touches Mosi I almost lose my shit. It is the first time I draw a shot from the bot. Luckily its aim is off, a dusty scope perhaps. I go motionless again. Wait for it to continue its slow sweep. Slowly, slowly, I undo the zip of the backpack, the sound of its opening lewd and out of place. With a bit of groping my hand closes on the gun. I pull it out, lift myself into a kneeling position as the sentry bot whips round, and we both fire at the same time. The bullet slams into me enough to spin me around and I fall across Mosi who grunts. I see the bot explode upside down though and breathe a massive sigh of relief. My eyes blur with tears as I note that Mosi is still alive and start trying to staunch both of our bleeding. I feel very tired, rolling the cloth around my shoulder and watching the slow red spreading stain hypnotises me. My eyes keep wanting to close.

I can hear an engine. I think it's coming from the town. I hope it's a traveller and not just someone coming to investigate a broken sentry bot. I'll just rest my eyes until they arrive ...

ABOUT PETER SUTTON

Pete Sutton has a not so secret lair in the wilds of Fishponds, Bristol and dreams up stories, many of which are about magpies. He's had stuff published, online and in book form, including a short story collection called A Tiding of Magpies (Shortlisted for the British Fantasy Award 2017) and the novel Sick City Syndrome.

He wrote all about Fishponds for the Naked Guide to Bristol and has made more money from non-fiction than he has from fiction and wonders if that means the gods of publishing are trying to tell him something. Pete is a member of the North Bristol Writers.

You can find him all over social media or worrying about events he's organised at the Bristol Festival of Literature, Bristol HorrorCon and BristolCon. On Twitter he's @suttope and he's published by Kensington Gore http://www.kensingtongorepublishing.com/pete-sutton/4591911186

https://petewsutton.com/
Twitter: @suttope

FOREVER NOON

by Harry Manners

"You said you were going for air," Anna said.

Carl Overmeyer stood in the doorway of their apartment and tried to hold onto his unthinking smile. "It's so beautiful out there. We spend too much time indoors, don't you think?" he said.

"Carl," Anna snarled. "You said you were going for air."

"I did. I got thinking about things, kind of lost track."

"I've been waiting hours. You're filthy. You're bleeding!"

"It was just a walk out of the city. There are still fields out there. Forests." He didn't mention his precipitous fall down an embankment.

Anna's expression wrestled the smile from his face. He hated her then, for bringing him back to stark reality.

She eyed him with the cold rapture of a snake preparing to strike. "I'm not doing this. You're trying to rile me. I'm not playing games today," she said.

Carl slammed the door. Silence fell over the apartment like a canvas sack.

They glared at one another.

"You can't do this every time you need a distraction. The day's going to keep coming around every year. You can't stop it," Anna said.

"I know it's going to keep coming, damn it! That's

why I went for a walk. Just let me get on with it."

"It's just another day," Anna said.

"Yeah. Sure. Just another day. Been enough of those," he muttered, ducking into the living room to stare at the wall.

The urge to scream clawed up out of nowhere, like it did sometimes. A physical need so strong it brought tears to his eyes, like a sneeze just averted.

His eyes moved over the wall, searching for distraction – he needed some distraction, for God's sake! – and recoiled when his gaze passed over framed photographs.

Their third date by the Ferris wheel on Long Beach pier, Anna with a stick of candy floss in her hand. A shot of them in Quito during the summer festival. Their twenty-fifth anniversary in a moldy motel in Missouri, when they had been penniless and on the move for a whole summer. Their fortieth anniversary, at Mount Everest base camp. Their fiftieth, grinning in zero gravity while taking a parabolic orbital flight. Their sixtieth...

The faces in the photos were all the same, unblemished, unwrinkled, unchanged.

"I made you a cake," Anna said. Her expression didn't soften as she gestured to the table, upon which sat a home-baked sponge. Twelve candles had been stuck in the top in a neat row, all melted down to nubs. Wax had spilled over the icing. Twelve candles burned down to nothing, but still aflame. A candle for each decade.

"Happy birthday, Carl," Anna said.

*

Anna lay behind Carl on the floor, curling an arm over him in the dark. They watched the rain run down the window panes. Their bed was untouched, neatly made.

"You haven't moved for hours," she said.

"I can't," he said.

"Why?"

"Just... one of those days."

He wondered if she would get mad and give him the cold shoulder for another week. They hadn't spoken since he let the cake she made go stale.

He inhaled sharply when her lips touched the nape of his neck, so soft that the little hairs sizzled down his back.

"Stay with me," she said.

With great effort he turned onto his back, to gaze at the dark outline of her face. "I'm here," he said.

"No you're not. You're hardly ever here anymore."

"I try to be." He hesitated. "You're gone most of the time, too."

She tightened. "It feels like I'm tumbling through trapdoors in the dark, and I can't stop."

He brushed her hair. Despite himself he gazed through her, not at her. It was so hard to actually look at anything. Sometimes it was hard to believe any of it was real; other times, like now, it was too painful to even remember they were real.

Had he really become so bored with life that even the phantasms of the subconscious and the wildernesses of hallucination could barely hold back the boredom?

"We could sign up for something off-world. Luna. The next shipment to Mars. We could start over." Anna's voice was thin, hardly there.

He didn't bother to answer. They lived by a code and it worked, had done for so long there was no reason to think it wouldn't keep on working forever, so long as they stuck to it... except that a tear had opened in the fabric holding him together, which widened a little more every time he looked inwards.

Imperceptibly widening, stretching, unravelling.

Rip... rip.... riipppp.

Anna rose from his chest. "What is it?"

"You always know."

"I can hear it. It sounds like grinding cogs in old clockwork."

He wet his lips. "We could stop, Anna. We could let it come and it would all go away."

She jerked. "Don't."

The warning in her tone was powerful enough to stall the conversation.

He stared at the two pockets of shadows where her eyes hid, and once again returned to the rain. "What do they think at night? The lowfolk? Knowing it's coming and not able to do a thing about it. They get a couple of measly decades grown up before it all sags and fades and falls apart. How do they get up and do it all, day after day, when time's so short? How do they keep themselves from screaming?"

Anna perched on the rug beside him, her lips pressed to her knee. "I don't know. At least they're alive. I'd rather be close to them instead of back in Paradise – back with them."

"Yes. Not with them."

"They'll find us eventually. They always do."

"Let them. I'm tired of running. What can they do?"

"They could try to make us go back."

"We won't. We're staying here. I want to be as close to what we used to have as I can..." He trailed off and sat up. Something about the way she angled her head snagged his attention. "You think as loudly as I do."

Her throat worked in the gloom.

"I don't want to go back either but maybe they're right. What if we took a little Honey, just to take the edge off? Time wouldn't hurt so much, for a little while."

22

"I'll never go back to being like that."

"I won't either. But we could do it just for a little while; rest up, so we can come back to this."

"It won't work that way. It never does. We take Honey and we'll be no different from them. How many years did it take us to get away from it even when we knew we had to?"

"I know! I know!" She whirled from him into darkness.

No matter how many times the sun arced over the sky, neither serenity nor wisdom ever came. Always it was the petty arguments, the long nights of talking by the window, the anger and fear and stupidity.

"We can't stay like this. You can't keep running away from me. You can't keep breaking, stealing, goofing off. It's picking me apart," Anna said somewhere out of sight.

Carl couldn't speak for a while. There was a ball in his throat and he could barely breathe. Eventually he croaked, "I'll find a way."

They lay there until the darkness began to withdraw and another day – another day – crept up upon them without mercy. Golden crepuscular light threw back the comforting shadows. They washed and ate breakfast in silence.

Not a single thought passed Carl's mind, just the unending desire to crawl through some magic portal into one of the photo frames on the wall, to that day on Long Beach pier, when the world still promised uncertainty ahead.

Carl shaved and jerked at his reflection. It seemed to him that his face had appeared suddenly, though he had been staring into the mirror for some time. He stood with his face bleeding, razor in hand, not sure his image had indeed been there only a moment before.

*

Herman Pondozza appeared in the hallway the next day. Slope backed, haggard and goat faced, a Frankenstein of a man. His enormous hands had the texture of sandpaper and bore calluses the size of coins, yet his face had the aquiline roundness of a man suited to being locked away in study.

"You're one of them from Paradise, ain't you?" he said. He frowned, sucking his mouth into a grimace at Carl's proffered hand, but his eyes twinkled. "One of them assholes, ain't you? One of them backward lizard-skinned cold-hearted bastard assholes." He slapped his hand into Carl's and gave it a crushing shake. "Good to meet you!"

Carl blinked, stunned. "I guess that's me," he said.

He and Anna had lived in the same apartment building for the last three years, and not once had anybody shown even a hint of guessing who they were – what they were. This old fart had known at a glance.

Carl croaked, "How did you know?"

"Name's Herman Pondozza. Call me Herm." He looked up and down the dilapidated corridor. "What a shitbucket. Good place, great place! Mrs Pondozza woulda chewed my ass right down the middle if she ever saw me in a place like this. Bet she's spinning in her grave like roast chicken on a spit." He peeled with laughter, which caused him to double over in a coughing fit, then he shook Carl's hand again. "Absolute craphole. Love it! Good a place as any to see this out."

"See what out, Mr Pondozza?"

"Please, Herm! I'm seein' out this whole business of fading away like a ghost in a B-movie showdown.

24

Shriveling up until I'm a prune in a box and they burn my ass out the chimneys. This whole ageing thing sucks, you know? No, I suppose you don't. Funny, that. Jeez, I bet that's a gas, getting up every morning and pissing like a horse and fucking and jumping jacks down the gym like it was nothing."

Carl waited. He braced himself to hurry back to Anna, to pack and move again. Once the news was out it always spread, and people stopped wanting them around.

Herman slapped his arm and laughed. "You look like you got a frog in your throat, bud."

Carl mouthed wordlessly. "W-w... How?"

"Ah, you got that way about you. Like you seen it all and you've got nothing to look out for. I got an eye for it, see. Worked the night shift in the Paradise kitchens back when they still used manpower instead of them damn automated systems. You know, in your fancy-pants restaurants where they use all the senses and make broccoli taste like caramel candy? I know you people when I see you. Tell me, Mr..."

"Carl. Just Carl."

"Carl, sure. Carl, tell me how you ended up in a place like this? I woulda thought it'd be crazy for somebody to leave a place set to give them everything until the sun dies and swallows the world up."

Electricity crackled in Carl's toes, the urge to run. "I, uh..."

"I gotta say it doesn't make a lick of sense to me, but you've got some years on me, I bet. Hell, I must be a kid compared to you. No way to tell, I suppose. I wonder how that feels, nobody knowing what generation you're from, what you grew up with, what cartoons you were watching as a kid. Wow, think of that!"

Carl backed away slowly. "Listen, I got to get back. I

said I wouldn't be gone long." It sounded even more pathetic out loud that it had sounded in his head.

Herman watched him a second then his enormous mangled hand alighted like a butterfly on Carl's forearm. "Ain't no problem. How about I walk back with you."

"Okay."

Carl bet he and Herman were about the same height, but with his curved spine Herman stood a head shorter. Yet Carl felt tiny, like an ant under the man's boot.

How's he doing this? I feel like I'm five-years-old clowning around in front of my Dad. How's that for messed up? I must have forty years on this kid.

"Where's your place? I don't remember anybody moving out lately," Carl said.

"Oh, I ain't got one of the apartments. No money left after Mrs Pondozza's cremation and sorting her affairs. The booths downstairs are good enough for my old bones." Herman laughed, eyes so alive it hurt to look at them trapped in his decrepit body.

Something snapped inside Carl. This man wasn't sleeping next to fifty other lowfolk, not in one of those booths where they stacked them ten high like battery chickens.

"Come with me. I insist," he said.

Herman raised his brows.

It took less than quarter of an hour to get back to Anna, talk her around, and move Herman's spare possessions into their apartment.

Herman laughed like a balloon with a hole in the neck until late in the afternoon. Then his withered undernourished body began shaking, and he coughed until he spat stringy spittle. While they looked on, baffled, he fell into a senseless torpor until morning.

"You know what you've done, don't you? He's too

alive, Carl. He'll make us feel too much. I don't know what will happen," Anna said.

"I know," Carl said. "But we had to do something."

They spent another sleepless night gathered on the sofa, watching Herman, horrified and fascinated.

*

Herman had been a suet chef, having worked his way up from pot-washer. He and his wife had borne a litter of four, done their time raising their family and then kicked back into the swing of a long middle age.

Things had gone downhill during the endless depressions late in the last century and the resource wars that followed. By then restaurants slid off the map and power cuts rolled across the former United States. They had been unlucky enough to hit later life just as the world changed fastest, when a tortured planet finally groaned and snapped and poured billions of people into the abyss.

Herman made sure his children scattered to the corners of the continent, in search of opportunity and better lives – praying they might escape the mega-slums popping up in Yosemite, along the shores of the Hudson, the ruins of the Mississippi delta, and dozens of other places.

For Herman and his wife, such long journeys belonged to yesteryear. They moved slow, like Great Depression Oakies on the back of relief transports and whoever would take them. They walked miles for handfuls of grain, had pretty much given up on finding a way out of their new hell, when they landed in a safety net they never expected: jobs as lowfolk in Paradise, one of the fortress spires that was home to the world's ageless one-percent.

Herman told his story blue lipped and pale, yet

animated.

Carl sat close to him, ready to catch him if he fell, enraptured by the man's failing body, the wrinkles, the effervescent, full consciousness trapped inside a traitorous bag of failing organs.

What might I look like if I didn't take my morning dose of anti-senescents?

He said, "So you worked in the kitchens?"

"Almost ten years. From sixty-four until seventy-three. Coulda gone on for another ten, if Norma hadn't faded so fast. Didn't matter that there ain't no doctors for normal folks now; she was sick only a day or two. After she passed, I just couldn't keep up. Like a switch flipped inside of me that said 'Well, your time's your time. Off this mortal coil you go!' How's that for rude?"

Carl smiled politely.

Anna bustled around them, touching the photo frames, watering the plants. It was as though she was unable to sit down. "What happened in the kitchens?" she said. Carl knew she didn't mean it to sound accusatory, but it did: what are you doing here?

If Herman picked up on it, he didn't show it. "Paradise ain't got no room for imperfection... Say, you ever have the duck confit with cranberry coulis and buttered asparagus?"

Carl shook his head. "No, I..."

"Yes," Anna said.

Herman slapped his leg and barked until he wheezed. "Good god, that was my dish. We all got one you see. There was a whole army of us making the same thing over and over. That dish that come up out of the chute into your room was right from my hands! Think of us being back there, same building but worlds apart; now here we are, like we were... like, equals or something."

He turned about. "It don't figure. Nobody would leave that behind." He frowned at them hard, and for the first time the twinkle in his eye dimmed. "It's not me who's out of place. What are you two doing here?"

Carl's mouth filled with cement. He looked to Anna for help and for a moment he thought he saw stitches binding her lips shut.

*

The amusement that was Herman faded as all fleeting excitements fade, and he became as much a part of their apartment as the furniture.

He refused help, showed little appetite, choked on his food often. Somehow he still managed to enjoy eating, slowly, masticating in the scrim of sunlight coming in through the smog-riddled clouds. It took up most of his morning.

Anna soon gave up fussing over him and went back to her studio in the spare bedroom. Carl used to love watching her, baffled by her exploits, the places she went in her head, the canvasses she produced in paroxysms of artistic fervor.

"You haven't been in here in months," he said, hovering by the door.

"I can't watch him," Anna said, cross legged on the floor, surrounded by sea of pop art cut-outs, antique paperbacks, and a few brightly colored infant's blocks.

Carl looked over his shoulder, but the apartment was empty. Herman had gone for one of his walks. At his pace, he would be some time. "Why?"

"I can't look at what he's becoming... coming undone. He's been here two weeks and he's already grown worse."

"He's old, Anna."

She laughed, brandishing a brush freshly dipped in red paint. The color startled him as much as the harshness of her voice. "He's a child compared to us. Just coming to know the world and how it works, what one could and should actually do with it, and now he's coming apart like an old sweater, and there's nothing he can do but watch – no! He has to live it."

Carl couldn't compete when she was like this; he didn't have an artistic side of his own.

Look at Anna in a vacuum and you'd expect her partner to have been born with a beret permanently attached to his head, spouting Baudelaire and Schrödinger in equal measure: some baguette-eating, sandal-wearing genius. Not Carl, whose greatest achievements had been stealing and stirring up petty trouble to keep ennui at bay.

"What's the matter with you? You're staring," Anna said.

Carl started. "Nothing. Just... doesn't he, you know, make you want to watch him? If he's going through it..."

"No. I don't want to experience that even once. Why would I want to watch it happen to somebody else?"

"It's part of being human, isn't it?"

"No, it's part of dying, and we don't die, Carl."

"Everything dies, eventually. We can still fall out a window, get sick... We're not going to live forever."

She didn't say anything for a long time, looking at her pictures. Carl knew that look. Looking but not seeing.

"Most days I want it to come and take me when I'm not paying attention. Just, gone. Then days like today I can't even think about it without shaking..." She broke off and muttered angrily, maybe at him, maybe at herself. She started painting, splashing angry great strokes over blank canvas, snarling lip held between her teeth. "Wiser. Wiser with time. Tsh! Wiser..."

Carl left her and waited for Herman. He was going to watch this. He didn't have a special place in the firmament to retreat to, found no solace in the thoughts and creations of people long turned to dust. All he ever had was the physical world of mountaintops and good food, and Herman was part of that world.

Herman was going to die, like all the people in their building and all the lowfolk.

Carl had watched them wink out like fireflies in the coming dawn, replaced by their children, and their children's children. The cycle would never end, but he and Anna and all the people in Paradise would endure.

"It can only end one way," Carl said to the dust motes floating around his head.

At some point he fell asleep, and dreamed of Herman walking a dark forest path, ever narrowing, and Carl followed in his footsteps, scared to look and scared to look away.

*

"You can't be in here!"

"I think you'll find I pay for this space. It belongs to me more than it does you. Now leave me with my son, dear."

"Don't you call me dear. We're both as ancient as bone dust, wench. Get out of my house!"

"We both know I'm not going anywhere until I speak to him. Go back to your scribbling."

A scowl, a slamming door. The sound of groaning leather as somebody sat.

Carl opened bleary eyes. The apartment was in gloom, the curtains drawn. The smog had been due to thicken in early afternoon, and Anna hated the colors of a poisoned sky.

He hoped Herman had returned from his walk. The chemicals would finish his lungs if he was caught out in it. Carl sat up, squinting. "Herman, is that you?"

"Hello, darling."

Carl paused. Silence wailed in his ears. "What are you doing here?"

"Children used to have respect for their mothers."

"I asked you what you were doing here."

Carl's mother loomed from shadow: perfect hooked nose, rosy cheeks, hair tightly bound in a bun atop her head. Not bad for a hundred-and-thirty-nine. People in Paradise could choose any age they wanted, moving along the timeline of life at will. Most, Carl and Anna included, chose the sweet spot between twenty-eight and thirty-five, but his mother had always opted for her late forties.

"I've come to fetch my son," she said.

"Sorry, he's not here. Try down the road."

"Don't play with me, Carl. I'm not leaving without you this time."

She held still as a marble carving, and he saw what he hoped not to: a glaze to her eyes. In the half-light, they were the black buttons of a child's doll, addled by the Honey of Paradise.

"You should see what's changed in Paradise. It's so different. I know you'd love it."

"That place never changes. Not ever." Carl sat back. "How long was it this time before you realized I was gone? A month? Six? Do you even remember the last time you came after us?"

She didn't move, didn't blink. Not a flicker of pain or outrage passed her face.

Carl pushed away memories of the smothering miasma with which Honey stuffed the senses. Everything seemed far away when you were dosed: slow and inconsequential and devoid of color.

He knew what kind of willpower it took to break the cycle, to feel, to know something is wrong and act on it.

If she's here it's because... because the real her, somewhere under this doppelganger, is screaming.

She drew a theatrical sigh. "I know you hate me, hate all of us. Your father has stripped you from his mind. You know what he's like. He can't take it. But I still care about you." A softness muscled onto her expression, so plastic that it made Carl cringe. "I love you, Carl. Come home with me."

"I'm not going anywhere." Carl stood and padded to the kitchen. He snatched a glance at the spare bedroom and saw the light coming under the door cut off by Anna's figure.

Go back to your happy place, Anna. You don't want to hear this again.

"Dad never noticed me in the first place." He never noticed you, either.

Carl poured himself a glass of orange juice and relied on the dark to shield him from her stare. "How is he?"

"Still alive. Still at his desk."

That was the way it had been for almost a century, like hideous windup clockwork: they rose, they ate, they watched shows and stewed in sense pods, Dad worked on his research, Mom barked orders to her committee, and Carl died a little more inside.

He could see it in his head as though he were back there now, living any of countless thousands of days.

Carl drank his juice. The glass shook on the way to his mouth.

"I've been tolerant, I've been patient. I've kept your accounts open and let our money drain out into these filthy backwaters where you insist on hiding, I've let you play out this little childish game of yours. I understand. I know what it can be like when you stop taking Honey. It does funny things to your mind. But all you have to do is start your dose again, and it'll all be better."

"You know as well as I do what Honey is. It's a lie, Mom. Every single person in Paradise is a ghost."

"We are happy, Carl!"

"It only takes away the emptiness. What it fills the gap with is much worse."

She smiled and sat straighter, a prim stance of irritation. "You don't know what you're saying. You're sick."

Carl scoffed, made his way back to the sofa. "You're the one who's sick. I remember what it feels like to enjoy so much bliss you don't feel anything at all. It's those sense pods, Mom, you're never out of them. Every sensation piped into you to distract you from the boredom. I get it. But you can only enjoy so many delicious meals, so many simulated epiphanies, so many earth-shattering orgasms. Eventually it's just boring. It's normal. You don't feel it at all." He forced himself to glance at her. "Even if you realize it you can't break out of it. Getting rid of Honey's fog is like crawling out of a well, gagged and bound. And when you finally work up the courage to stop and walk away, the real world is so cold and bleak and lifeless that it takes years to start feeling things for real. I'll never be like that again."

"You can't live out here. It's not enough. You'll go crazy."

"You would go crazy, Mom. You never figured out how to live properly. Anna and I, we've found ways. Anna has her work, and I have her."

He didn't mention the crushing boredom that might have already killed him if Herman hadn't come along.

34

"This has gone on long enough. If I have to I'll freeze your accounts."

"We'll manage."

"You'll starve!"

"Maybe."

Her mouth twitched, the first sign of something stirring under the surface. "You're still just a little boy. You have no idea what I protect you from. You pretend you're playing the bohemian beggar out in the wastes, but you're still as much a part of Paradise as any of us."

"Freeze the accounts and we'll find out."

She sniffed violently and stood. "You will come home with me and stop this nonsense!"

"You've come after us... how many times now? You know what Einstein said about repeating the same thing over and over and expecting a different result?"

"Don't talk to me that way!"

"Are you mad because I won't come home, or because no matter how much they adjust your dose, you still end up feeling something?" He nodded to her white knuckles, bunched over her handbag. "It never goes away, does it? Not totally. And you can't stand knowing I'm out here looking for a way out."

The war inside her played out before Carl's eyes: someone he loved, trapped, fighting to the surface, tethered to the depths by a century of denial, habit, and a parade of artificial chemicals.

To his genuine horror, her eyes reddened and tears splashed onto the carpet. She had never wept, not in all the times she had chased him.

"Please, Carl," she gasped. "I can't. I can't stand being back there all alone. Your father hasn't spoken to me in years. I don't think he even knows we exist anymore."

Carl couldn't meet her eye. He parted the curtains,

looking out into the smog. "That's how he copes. I knew that long before I stopped taking Honey."

"Please, Carl. If those accounts are frozen and you lose your way, there won't be a next time. You'll be just another lowman. Those people die like cockroaches."

Carl stared at the slums outside, inhabited by souls allowed to persist so they could prop up gold-plated towers like Paradise dotted over the globe. He stared for long that the sounds of the building around him decomposed into the clanking and arguing of the other tenants, his mother's tight fuming, Anna's breathing in the next room.

"I want you to leave and never come back, Mom," he said.

"You don't mean that." She was standing, clutching her bag.

"We'll clear out of here by the end of the month. We won't trouble you for money anymore. Go back to your Honey." He fixated on the orange, preternatural light through the window. "Say hi to Dad for me."

He expected the door to slam, but he never heard it close at all. She must have pulled it to, softly, as she might have in another century as Carl had lain in a crib and her youth hadn't been a lie.

Some time later Anna appeared and rested her head on his shoulder. They watched the world together, breathing, blinking. Whistles signaled shift-change in the factories, and the building reverberated with people coming home to meagre meals, family arguments, and small amusements. Short lives being lived, not remembered; experienced, not mourned.

Herman came back near dark, his skin pale and translucent. They tried to make him rest but he wouldn't give up his schedule. He would soon be gone.

*

"We can't take everything with us. What do you want to keep?" Anna said.

They stood in the living room, looking around the apartment. They always tried to be Spartan with their homes, but when it came to this point their personal effects seemed to be overflowing.

"Nothing. We'll be fine," Carl said. "Do you want anything?"

"No. We'll give it to the neighbors." An ugly curl snagged Anna's lip. "We never manage to get away from Paradise, do we? It's always ends up this way, like an echo. Nobody in this building can afford drapes like ours, real wood floors, air filters."

Herman came in from his walk and settled on the sofa, wheezing. He trembled constantly now.

"You shouldn't wander so far. If you fall..." Carl said.

"If I fall, I'll die on the damned floor, taking my walk like I want," Herman said, spitting into the bedpan they kept by the sofa. "I can't even get to the elevator no more, anyway. Make do with shuffling up and down the hall and that's good enough. At least I get the view."

"Some view," Anna said.

"It's my city and I love it, shithole or not."

Carl sat in the armchair across from him. "We have to go. Rent's due in three days."

"Yeah, I know." Somehow, Herman managed to wink.

"We're going far." Carl paused, thinking, trying to work himself up to saying his piece, but Herman waved him down.

"I'm not going goin' anywhere now, so don't fret. My time's up."

Anna shook her head by the kitchen counter. "Aren't

37

you angry? Afraid?"

"Of course I am! Angry as hell. I'm not done with this world. Never saw what's out there, never learned a damn thing, never had sex with two women at once, never smoked a joint. But a man's time is his time and I'm getting square with it. You've got no obligation to me. I'll say thank you and goodnight."

*

Carl packed a box of essentials. Clothes, anti-senescent meds – the only things they could not do without, which kept them young –, electronic devices, a little preserved food.

Everything else was going to their neighbors. An estate agent came by, trawling a family of nine in her wake.

"Nine people in this place," Anna said under her breath after they left. "Nine."

Anna retreated into her painting, agonizing for hours over a handful of strokes. The forms she produced were anti-form, anti-meaning. Something too raw for aesthetic or coherence.

"How do you want to do it this time?" she said over dinner. "We could take a mystery bus again."

Last time it had been Milwaukee they had left behind, and at the coach station they had taken the first bus they saw. They ended up in the remotest corner of Montana, where people had shot daggers from their eyes and wouldn't sell them a slice of bread. They wandered down to Reno from there, camping rough and hitch-hiking.

They expected it to be romantic and genuine, like something out of a Kerouac novel. It had been an awful time: hungry and tired and cold in a senseless wilderness.

But of all the falsehoods, Carl thought maybe it had been closest to what might have been contentment.

"That's it," Carl said.

"What?"

Carl dropped his fork and went to their remaining box of possessions. He tore it open and poured everything into the waste basket. He hesitated, fished out their meds and IDs, and pocketed them.

Anna didn't say a thing, just watched as he returned to the table and resumed eating.

"We go with what we have and nothing else. We keep moving," Carl said.

"And what? Live off other people's kindness?"

"Why not?"

"The world we read about in books doesn't exist."

"What time we have will be worth it." He reached over the table to take her hand.

Anna didn't move. At last she said, "Okay."

He smiled. "I can't believe we never thought of it before." He squeezed her hand. "Do you want to do this?"

Another silence. "We don't have a choice."

"Don't say it like that. This is our decision. We decide to live."

"Okay."

They finished eating. That night Herman hacked his lungs out on the couch and once more they lay awake in the darkness.

Carl battled mental flashes of how Anna's face had looked over dinner. Her expression haunted him: not happiness or relief but fear, capping a well of rage.

*

Carl researched bare essentials over breakfast, writing them down on a pad, with a real pen. In a moment of madness, he had decided that his one vintage notebook and pen would be his sole source of information from now on. He would write down what they needed and short out his implant. The internet and all its noise would be just be a distraction on the road.

He was clumsily scrawling the locations of anti-senescent drug banks when Herman came to the table, breathing hard.

Carl kept writing, glad for the company but concentrating on forming letters. Carving them out with the pen had an unappealing initial crudeness, but after a while he had relaxed into the tactile pleasure.

He was enjoying forming the looping l in Corvallis so much that when Herman spoke, it took a beat for his words to sink in.

"Time for me to go, Carl."

Carl's hand kept moving for a few more moments, then his l jerked off into a jagged spur and he looked up. "What?"

"Time's up."

Carl wrestled back the urge to say all the things one thinks they should say whether they really want to or not.

"It's been a pleasure," he said eventually.

Herman's eyes twinkled behind the cocoon of frailty that had consumed him. "It's a good day for it." He nodded to the window and the sunlight streaming in.

"It is. The smog's thin today. Where will you go?"

"I don't know. Wherever these old legs take me."

Carl resisted lending a hand as Herman struggled to his feet.

The old man wept from the pain of standing and held onto the table, wheezing.

He won't fade away, he isn't gasping for another last moment. He's going out on his own terms...

An overwhelming surge of jealousy swept over Carl as Herman ambled to the door and put on an old dusty fedora.

Herman turned with his hand on the doorknob. A weak smile peeked over his shoulder, accompanied by a pair of eyes young as any child's, just as afraid and mischievous.

Carl dashed Goodbye, Herman from the tip of his tongue and instead said, "Travel safe, kid."

"Make it count," was all Herman said, then vanished through the door and was gone.

Carl sat at the table until Anna stirred from the bedroom, bedheaded.

"You always look beautiful after you've slept."

"I look like I've been dragged backwards through a bush," she said groggily. "Sleeping gets harder the less you do it. Where's Herman?"

Carl went back to his notepad. The old man's absence pressed at him like a physical pressure, and suddenly he was more desperate than ever to be rid of the lights and circuitry that bonded him to cyberspace, to unlife and everything that divided his attention.

Anna said nothing. She sat watching his unpracticed scrawling, then she erupted from the table and kicked her chair across the room.

Carl started, but no words came. She paced the living room, pulling anything loose to the floor, then yanked fistfuls of her tangled hair.

"He did it right. He didn't run," Carl said.

"There is nothing brave or romantic about dying, Carl!" she bellowed. "Haven't you figured that out by now? All this extra time the drugs bought you and you still don't know that? Life is all there is and after that it's just nothing, so where's the sense in running to it?"

Carl let the silence hang. He closed his pad. "Nobody runs to it. It comes. I'm not doing it anymore: grasping a few more moments at the price of everything we were."

"It's not the same. We don't age, Carl."

"I know. But that's no way to think. Being afraid of what will eventually come, wondering about fate or destiny or worth or any of that crap. What's the point of all this time if we don't use it for living?"

For a horrible moment she had his mother's face, and he hardly recognized the woman standing in front of him. He tamped down the urge to run.

Anna wilted like a flower in a cold snap. She stalked to the spare room and slammed the door.

Carl ate dinner alone and went to bed angry. He tossed and turned until the anger ebbed, then his thoughts turned to Herman, sure to be gone by now.

What had been the old man's his last thoughts? Did refusing to run make it easier, in the end, when the last moment danced up from the ether? Did it tame that final moment of fear?

*

Carl took his pills at the counter in the bleak pre-dawn light. Anna had been in the spare room all night. He would give her some space today. Something was close now, and whatever it was scared him.

A knock sounded at the door just as the first fingers of sunlight rained onto the carpet. A haggard, unshaven envoy stood in the hall, and told him that a Herman Pondozza had been found dead at the dockyards.

There would have been a view of the harbor, Carl

thought. A holiday memory Herman had shared with his wife, perhaps? A childhood summer vacation goofing around the fish markets?

Whatever it had been, Carl hoped it had been worth it.

"How did you find us?" he said.

"This address was sown into Mr Pondozza's shoes. I assume they're yours? If you want to report them stolen, I can get them recovered for you..."

"No, no," Carl said. He thanked the envoy, gave him a tip he and Anna couldn't afford, and returned to the counter.

He cried for a while, silent easy tears, then made some more notes. He looked over the pages and made sure he had everything.

"Time to wake up," he said aloud, and went to the bathroom. Taking his time to remember the tutorial video he had seen on the internet, he removed the cover on his implant, just behind his left ear. Careful not to dislodge anything that would need medical attention, he removed the micro-battery and closed it up.

The device was only an external transmitter; the implant consisted of a cloud of devices throughout his skull and the rest of his nervous system. It would still operate off his body's electric impulses for a while, but eventually the power would run down, and his link to the outside world would fade.

He refused to be afraid, but he felt the loss, like somebody had cut off his feet. At the same time, relief flooded through him. He didn't have to fight to keep the endless noise of the net at bay.

Anna came out of the spare room at lunchtime and ate an entire box of cereal. She didn't say a word, just watched him. She smiled, and he smiled back at her, immensely relieved.

She'll be back tomorrow. I'll wait for her. God knows she's waited for me enough times.

He peeked into the spare room and caught a glimpse of red and blue splashes of paint. Torn pages from antique paperback books littered the floor.

She finished eating and went back into the room.

"I'll be here if you need me," Carl said.

She paused, her face just visible. She focused on his feet. "Okay."

"I'll see you later."

She nodded again, eyes doughy. The door closed and Carl listened to the violent slap of her brush against canvas until late in the afternoon.

*

Moving day. Carl found himself smiling as he cooked a hot breakfast. He even whistled as he fried the imitation eggs.

He touched his notebook often, tucked in his back pocket. Excitement prickled his belly, as though he were taking his first excursion into the big unknown.

He took the plates of fake bacon and eggs, toast, pancakes and orange juice to the table and went to the spare room for Anna.

He was still whistling when he opened the door and his gaze found flesh, white and lifeless as stone.

Carl might have screamed. He wasn't sure. The floor was suddenly very far away and his body turned to rubber. The thing on the floor stared unseeing, and for a time he too didn't see.

His eyes wandered to the unfurled hands that had painted and crafted for over a century. Beside them lay the bottle of Honey that had been kept locked away under the bed.

The doses in Paradise were automated, carefully controlled through a pneumatic injector. The bottle held just regular pills, emergency doses. It was empty.

"How could you be so stupid?"

He kneeled beside her and cradled her head in the crook of his elbow. A thread of congealed spittle coated the corner of her mouth, but otherwise she seemed relaxed, pensive.

He put his forehead on hers. "We were almost free.

Come on, now. Enough games. Enough." He scrambled for strength but his body betrayed him, leaking hot tears.

He sat back and braced himself against the wall, hugging his knees. Anna's canvas still perched on the easel, without form or intent, the smearing of some doped asinine creature.

"What were you trying to do?"

Anna stared at the ceiling. Not playing dead: dead.

He sat rocking until at last she did speak to him. She didn't move her lips but he heard her nonetheless.

"I needed to not feel again. I couldn't wait," she said. She sounded calm, befitting her thoughtful expression.

He crawled over to her and brushed a stray hair from her cheek. "It was today. Maybe it would have worked." He glared accusingly at the empty bottle. "You never helped anybody."

Then the bottle spoke to him too, aloof. "We do what we were made to. And you're wrong, Carl. You can always come back. Mom, Dad, Paradise, Honey, the delicious food, the sense pods, all of it. All you have to do is come home and be with us again, forever."

A receding echo, down and down, forever.

Carl clasped Anna's hand and tried to hold onto what

he had had a few minutes before: anticipation of the road and a path unknowable, leading to ruin or salvation and who knew what else? Maybe Herman was somewhere out there waiting for them, and everyone else they had known and lost. Maybe the answer waited for them and all they had to do was chase it.

With a pop it all vanished. No hitch-hiking, no contented misery walking through the rain in the middle of God's nowhere, no answers. Just this thing before him and his own unuttered screams.

He stood jerkily and without touching the thing, retreated to the door. "You were always the lucky one out of the two of us," he said, and closed the door.

He wandered to the sofa, in stillness now alien to him without his implant's internet feed; a world suffused with deafening silence.

Carl dug out their old tablet, hesitated one last time, and made a call.

*

The streets ran black with the grime of generations. The city had been quirky not long ago, a playground to distract him from decades-long boredom. A holding pen for the lowfolk; stylishly degenerate, almost Parisian in its romantic decrepitude. A place to battle ennui with wine and sex and art.

Now it was changed.

They were all real: the children playing with sticks in mud, the workers with thick calloused hands and lungs scarred by factory chemicals, the parents huddled in doorways and under lean-tos, wrapped tight in blankets and cooking meagre broth. Lives without chance of revolution. There was no room for sadness or dreams here. There was only living until the living was done, then there was not.

It all poured in without filter into the gaping hole in Carl's side where Anna had been.

The shadow of a gargantuan tower loomed over him; the doors of Paradise lay ahead. With tongue thick and cheeks red, he announced himself to the cold metal eyes imbedded over the doors.

The worst thing was how easy it was to return: a momentary scan, a one-word voice confirmation, and the great doors popped ajar; a conspiratorial gesture that said come, quick, before the rabble come calling.

Carl shivered as he stepped over the threshold and the air changed, cold and clean and sanitized. Soft overhead lights, miniature oak trees and ferns reaching from island oases out into seas of polished marble. All of it comprised the lustrous bosom of Paradise.

After being out with the lowfolk, it was like staring into the sun.

He didn't pass another citizen for minutes in the glossy vastness. Only lowfolk servants, faceless and hunched over. He forced himself not to scream for them to run.

Paradise was a lifeline to these lucky few. Perhaps a few of them would live to die a good death, like Herman.

Swallowing his disgust he ascended the many elevators through hundreds of stories. No guards came, nobody questioned his presence, nobody even glanced at him. Every door opened to his touch. This was his home, his birthright.

All the while he nursed a tender half smile. None of this was really happening, after all. How could it?

He and Anna were flying along the west coast on account of some charitable truck driver, eating canned beans and finding themselves in the dirt. Anna sketched masterpieces right alongside god-awful junk, and she let the scrapbook get chewed up in the bottom of her bag because it was the making that mattered.

Then Carl knocked on a hardwood door marked Overmeyer, and the bubble of fantasy popped.

The rapid patter of feet and stifled sobs sounded behind the door, which wrenched open and his mother stood before him.

There was no greeting, no words were exchanged. The condo was quiet and dark and smelled of rich foods.

Carl hesitated before crossing the threshold.

Should I go to Anna's parents? Should I tell them?

No. Let them go on with their lies. They probably won't notice she's gone for years, anyway.

He sat with his mother around the coffee table and she pushed a dose of Honey across to him.

"No," he said.

"Yes," she muttered. Her face was rounder, flabbier. She had been gorging herself.

"I'm not going back to that."

"We have to. I tried coming off it. I wanted to come with you, but I–" She paused, cocked her head in a paranoid glare, and was silent.

A distant clacking and muttering came from the study upstairs that was the sole domain of Steven Overmeyer.

Carl's father was working, as he had always worked. Last time they had seen one another, his father had tried to order a cup of green tea from Carl, mistaking him for a pet lowman.

"He's getting worse. I tried to speak to him yesterday. I hadn't taken a dose in days. No sense pod sessions. I was so lonely. I just wanted to speak to him, and he..." Tears filled her eyes. She put her injector to her elbow and shot a dose of Honey.

She scootched over the sofa to take Carl's hand, stroking his knuckles, tugging his fingers. "I'm glad you're home, darling. It'll all be better now that you're here."

Carl watched her in silence. He shouldn't have come. Already she had demonstrated it was doomed to fail yet again. She had come off Honey because even she hadn't been able to stand its diaphanous veil of fake nirvana.

Run. Run now before it's too late. You'll be right back where you started. Without Anna, you'll never have the strength to break free.

That was so. But where else was there to go but into the past? That was the only place he could find Anna now.

We were so close.

He took the injector and in the reflection of the metal was a last glimmer of what might have been, but never was.

"It's good to have you home, darling," his mother said.

Already her hand stroking his fingers felt better. His father's clacking and muttered dictation became a mellifluous symphony. The light grew rich, glowing into him, filling him.

Later he made his way to a sense pod, where Anna lay beside him. Floating, staring, he waited for time itself to dilute and stretch, and took another dose of Honey.

ABOUT HARRY MANNERS

Harry is an indie sci-fi and fantasy author, living in London and studying for a doctorate in physics. His previous works include the apocalyptic fantasy trilogy, The Ruin Saga, blending a stark post-apocalyptic world with a strange supernatural war.

www.harrymanners.net
Twitter: @harry_a_manners
Facebook:www.facebook.com/officialharrymanners

ANOTHER PLACE

by Mike Evis

"That's the lifeboat?" I gasped. "Are you serious? That thing?"

It didn't look much; it was nothing more than a long, thin metal tube.

My father shrugged. I hated it when he did that. I knew the inevitable sort of phrase he'd follow it with.

"It's all I had to work with. It'll do. We don't have much time, Zak."

"I don't see how all five of us can fit in there. Couldn't you build something bigger? There's barely room for one—"

"I had to work fast. We have to go one at a time, that's the way it works. It's self-navigating, you see —the lifeboat takes you, drops you off, and then it comes back for the next person. It's all automatic, you don't have to do anything, it'll return by itself. But I couldn't make it any larger."

I shook my head. My father and his crazy schemes. Why, he couldn't even build a proper lifeboat. Room for just one person? This was madness.

"It doesn't even look watertight. Imagine, one big wave—"

For a split second, I saw a half smile play across my

father's face. I couldn't work out why he looked so amused. Was he playing a huge joke on us all? But before he could speak my mother cut in.

"Stop it. Stop complaining, Zak. You know we have to leave this place. Your father's put a lot of work into this. Don't be so ungrateful. We're only thinking of you and your sisters."

"Trust me," said my father, "it'll be fine."

I noticed a worry line appear on his forehead.

My two sisters looked at each other. Terri, the eldest, scowled.

"What about my friends?" she asked. "This is so typical. You never think of us. We're all going to be split up. I'll never see them again."

"Now look what you've done," my mother said to me.

Turning back to Terri, she said, "This is for the best. We have to go."

"I think Zak's scared," said Sammi, my little sister. "Too frightened to try it out. You're a coward, Zak."

"Why you cheeky – of course I'm not."

"Yes you are. If you're not scared, why don't you go first?"

"Bet you wouldn't."

"Zak's frightened."

"No, I'm not. I just think–"

"Be quiet, the two of you," hissed Terri.

"Someone has to go first," said my father. "Will you do that, show your sisters the lifeboat's safe?"

"Yes," I said. "I'm not scared. And if it gets me away from her–" I pointed at Sammi. She poked her tongue out.

Before I set out, my father warned me of the dangers. The people were strange and they were violent; their customs were not ours. I wouldn't understand their language. He explained why there was no other way. We had to leave. And I must be careful once I arrived. I should wait where the lifeboat left me for the rest of them to arrive.

The first day was long. The lifeboat had washed up on the shoreline of a great river, next to a wild place of grass, shrubs and small trees. I half-imagined some mythical wild animal like a tiger or lion walking out of the shrub land. There were so many plants I marvelled to see their sheer numbers, all the different shapes and colours, all the varied shades of green. I'd never seen anything like it. Our land wasn't like this; it was harsh, hot and dusty, and what plants there were struggled to grow amidst the dried up soil and the relentless heat.

Absorbed by this strange and wonderful place, I was shocked when I breathed in the air. How strange and unpleasant it tasted, not like the hot dry desert air I was used to, or the cool freshness of the air indoors, out of the sun. Instead this was almost unbreathable, so filthy it made me cough, it was so thick with dirt and impurities. It was worse than the worst sandstorm. How could people live here breathing air like that? I was unsteady on my feet after the journey, so I stood for a moment, trying to ignore that filthy air but it was hard not to be aware of its taste every time I breathed in.

As I brushed my finger past a vividly coloured purple bush, I gasped as a sharp pain went through my fingertip, and I saw a trickle of blood run down my hand. A sharp thorn next to the flower I had grazed had pierced the skin. Fascinated, and yet horrified, I realised what my father meant when he told me this was a violent place. I froze – what if the fierce animals I had imagined here weren't so mythical after all? This wasn't a good sign.

What could the people in such a place be like?

Gazing around in amazement, the blood on my finger starting to dry, I decided to explore, despite my father telling me not to wander off. I wasn't going to go far. I could easily find my way back. But as I trampled through thick grass, pushing aside thick fronds that groped at me on either side, I came to some rotten and cracked fencing with wide gaps where the fence was broken. Forcing my way through, the wood easily splintered and broke apart. And I found myself in another world, a confusing, crowded place of noise and immensity. Vast, ugly buildings reached high up into the sky, poking at it like the fat fingers of a giant. They were tall and brutal, in sharp angular shapes and grey stone, so unlike the delicate minarets and towers that graced the skies of our abandoned ancient cities. And different as well to the simple houses of wood and stone in our settlements, that stood no more than a storey or two, blending in with the landscape. Here there was no beauty, no craftsmanship, just brash arrogance.

The people, too, looked downtrodden and unhappy, no smiles on their faces as they scurried along the pavements, spurred on by some unseen taskmaster. As they hurried past, I noticed their strange clothes, the sort I'd only seen in pictures, so utterly unlike the loose fitting colourful robes we wore. Now I saw why my father had unearthed that trunk of clothes and started rooting through it, handing me garments to try. The baggy pair of leg coverings I wore was close to what I saw the men – and women – were wearing, though theirs were far tighter. My wool tunic too was outwardly similar to theirs. What did astonish me was the skimpy clothing of the women. I stood staring the first time I saw a woman, her legs completely bare, walking towards me. My sisters would never dream of walking around like that. And no one covered their heads either. I wondered if I would ever get used to it.

Strange and noisy vehicles rushed at high speeds through the wide thoroughfares between the buildings, belching clouds of smoke and fumes at terrifying speeds. There were so few of us now that days might go by before we'd see anything on the road other than people walking or cycling past. And when we did, it would be something simple and slow moving like a cart, not these huge monsters. We had no use for speed or power. You could stand and linger and stop to talk in the middle of the road, the roads were so quiet. But here it was different and in the midst of all this hubbub and commotion, I struggled to make sense of it all. There was something deeply depressing about the place, like some awful nightmare.

I had worried I would stand out at once among these people. What would they do when they spotted me? But I was invisible to them. I looked like them, and they looked like me. They hardly noticed me. I blended in with the crowd: with my white skin, my short hair. We were all human, after all.

As I walked further down the street, and overheard people talking, I couldn't understand a single word they said, just as my father thought. "It's a shame, but they stopped teaching the language before I was born. It doesn't matter. I'm sure we'll pick it up once we're there."

I felt driven to keep walking, further and further from the fence where I'd entered the city, gazing all around me. After some time the street opened up to reveal a view stretching out to show endless streets and buildings below, occasional green spaces too. In the distance, a faint haze hung over it all. How large was this city? Did it ever end? I was mesmerised. I kept walking further along the street, and tried to keep my eye on the sun to try and check my direction, but the sun was often hidden behind the tall buildings that kept the thoroughfares in shadow.

After I'd walked some way, branching off every now and again to explore a new way leading left or right, I had a sinking feeling. I wasn't sure how far I'd walked or which way I'd come. Without the sun to direct me, I was lost. I should have stayed put. I was supposed to be there for my parents, and Terri and Sammi. I had to find my way back. Panic overcoming me, I started to run, but I wasn't sure where I was running. I knocked into people, hearing them cursing at me, but in words I didn't understand. I ran and I ran, taking huge gulps of air that tasted sickening until, exhausted and unable to breathe the fumes any more, I was forced to stop, tears streaming down my face. I sank down to the pavement, hunkered down against the side of a building. I stopped myself crying by thinking of my sisters and how they would laugh at me, but then I just cried some more.

The huge wheeled vehicles thundered and roared past continually, thickening the air with their stink. It didn't seem to bother the people walking past at all. I'd never seen so many people in all my life. How could there be so many? And how, with that many people, could you ever know them all? It was hard to imagine so many of them, all living in the same place. Where I came from, such numbers just didn't exist. There were so few of us left. We were the last.

The sun sank beyond the deep canyons of the buildings. I'd been there for hours. I suddenly felt hot, my heart pounding with fear. I began to give up hope. I would never get back to that place, and if I didn't, I would might never find my family again. What if they had arrived hours ago in that wild place, and found me gone? What would they have thought? Then darker thoughts came. The lifeboat was experimental. Could there be something wrong with its programming? If only I had waited as I'd been instructed.

Occasionally people came up to me. Perhaps I was no longer as invisible as I thought. They jabbered away in their strange guttural tongue. At first they spoke quickly and urgently, then slower and slower, until finally, exasperated, they shouted at me and strode off in annoyance.

One older man in his fifties stopped and stared at my garments, then smiled. I'd tried my best to make sure my clothes blended in, but I hadn't got them quite right. The baggy trousers I wore were too loose. He beckoned to me, an enigmatic smile on his face, repeating the same sounds over and over. Warily, I remembered my father's words. "Be very careful. Remember, their customs are not our customs."

I hadn't understood that at the time – how could that be? Surely our rules and ways were, well, universal, weren't they? There couldn't be any other way. Now I saw there might be.

As my father said, "Compared to us, they are so primitive. Always fighting, even amongst themselves. That's what led to all the trouble." This was no place to stay but if I couldn't find the place where I'd landed...

Eventually, unexpectedly, the man suddenly lashed out at me with his hand, striking my face, and then kicked me in the shin. I gasped in pain. He kicked me again and sauntered off, shaking his head.

What kind of mad place was this? These people were barbarians. And where were my family? They would never find me now. I felt wretched and alone. I began to shiver as the temperature dropped. It was no place to stay, here in this place where two huge thoroughfares converged, where you could be attacked by lunatics. I looked round. The sun had gone down, but it was not dark at all. Huge lights hung high above the streets illuminating them, and other bright lights blazed all around from gigantic windows and doorways in the buildings all around. It was almost as bright as day. People crowded the pavements, even though it was evening, but now there was an edginess: an undercurrent of violence and menace. I had to get away but where? If only I could find the wilderness again but which way was it? It could be anywhere. I'd never find it in the semi-darkness.

It was no place for my sisters, I thought, as young men swaggered and staggered down the street, spilling into the road fighting, momentarily halting the vehicles that still hurtled past. Groups of young women, wearing skimpy clothing, ran around shrieking and screaming at each other. If they knew – I stopped myself. That was another thing my father had impressed on me. I must not tell anyone here where I was from. It was too dangerous. There was no knowing what might happen. "They're so... uncivilised," he said. "What they don't understand, they can only destroy. They might well kill us all. Don't tell them anything."

I didn't really follow him then, but now I saw what he meant. Hot tears ran down my cheeks again. I'd failed them all. I should have waited, and we would all have been reunited. Instead, I had to be curious and wander off. I made up my mind what to do. I walked down the street rapidly, looking for somewhere, anywhere would do, to hide away until dawn, somewhere safe and secluded. I needed to make sure I survived the night.

Once it was morning it would be easier to work out where the lifeboat had dropped me.

I ducked down a narrow alleyway between two high buildings so tall they made me dizzy. Piled high with sacks and metal containers, the alley stank of decay and rotten food. I didn't like the smell but at least I'd be tucked away. I sat down heavily on a sack, halfway down the alley, far away from the street. Above, clouds of vapour escaped from the buildings into the dark sky, as if the buildings were alive and breathing. The sky was completely clear and through the vapour a few stars twinkled dimly above. I searched desperately for familiar constellations, but the light from the street was too bright, and the gap of sky was too small to make them out. Perhaps it was as well. I probably wouldn't find any of them anyway such a long way from home.

Stretching out, I made myself more comfortable, resting my foot on another sack of rubbish, but it didn't seem very stable and began to shift. Suddenly, to my horror, the sack shook violently and rose up as I slid to one side. The sack split and gave. Cans, boxes, and rotten meat spilled everywhere – and a filthy figure, muttering to itself, clothes splattered with dirt, pushed through, covered in debris. I didn't hang around. I ran down the alleyway, desperate to get out.

Now the street didn't seem so threatening. It was only as I emerged into the light of the street that I realised the figure in the rubbish was someone in the same situation as me. Just someone needing somewhere to sleep. I didn't have to fear them.

I thought of my family again. They could be out there right now looking for me but there was nothing I could do right now. I still had to find somewhere safe to stay the night. Scurrying quickly down the street, shrieks, angry cries and urgent voices all around me, I looked for another alleyway to hide away in. I found one a few streets away, narrower than the other with less rubbish. I walked up to the end of the alley, finding a spot behind some discarded cardboard boxes. I didn't see anyone else. It was darker, but my eyes soon adjusted. I was far from the street and its disturbing noises, though there was still the occasional unsettling sound coming from outside. The sky was little more than a small strip between the two buildings: a few stars scattered in the sky like discarded jewels from my sister's necklace. I would not sleep, I knew, yet, as I leaned my back against the hard side of a building and felt its warmth from the heat of the day, a sudden weariness settled on me.

Strange dreams came in the night: dreams of walking through a desert land like ours, then coming to a great ocean that stretched out before me forever. Colours swirled and I saw the lifeboat again, drifting helplessly, and my sisters and my parents. I called to them, but they did not hear. Would I only ever see them again in dreams? Was I lost to them for good?

The sun was high, shining down from a pure blue sky above the canyon when I woke with a start. It had been daylight for hours. There was no time to waste. I had to find the green place again. I scrambled to my feet, and walked out of the alley onto the street, and searched for the place where the two thoroughfares met. It was farther along than I realised. The jostling crowds confused me. Could I be sure it was the same place? And even if it were, how would I find where the lifeboat had landed?

I wandered up and down. The brutal buildings, the teeming masses of people, the heavy rumble of the vehicles that roared down the streets, left me wearied and worn out. There was no sign of that little wild area of greenery where I had first encountered this city. Had I imagined it? I felt like giving up – but if I did that I would never see my family again, I knew. Leaning up against a bare, hard wall, I looked around carefully. I didn't recognise anything. Panic rose. The streets, the buildings, the people – they all looked the same. It could have been anywhere in the city.

Despair gripped me. The sun was drifting towards the middle of the afternoon now and I had spent half the day fruitlessly searching. I would never find that little wilderness. It was useless. I turned and walked back down the street. I no longer had any idea of where I was, and I no longer cared. Then I saw what looked like the top of a tree, poking out from behind – hang on, that was a fence, wasn't it? Was this it? I could hardly bear to look. Had I found it? Yes, this had to be the place I had knocked through the fragile fencing and walked out to explore the city. I squeezed through the gap, and found myself back in the wild green oasis of calm, the bustle of the city held at bay.

Walking through tall grass, shoving aside brambles, I looked for the lifeboat. There was no sign of it but the grass was crushed where I had dragged it up from the shore line. There were no other traces in the grass, no trails except the one I had made yesterday – or was it the day before? Time itself was becoming uncertain. How long had I been here? It felt like days.

My family wasn't here. It was the meeting place. This was where the lifeboat would return. They weren't coming. They were never coming. Something was wrong. The lifeboat had left me stranded, far from everything and everyone I knew, amongst these strange people.

I told myself to calm down. There had to be a simple

explanation. Maybe they had already arrived and gone to look for me. Maybe they got the place wrong. Perhaps the lifeboat had drifted off course slightly. They could be in the next street. Or across on the shores of another sea. There was no way of knowing. I might never see them again. Tears began to run down my face, and a salt taste like the sea came into my mouth. I realised how hungry, how thirsty and utterly alone I was.

The craft was experimental, but my father had been reassuring, "The systems are all automated. There's nothing to go wrong. Plus it's got a return mechanism. I've checked it all over."

But there was no margin for error. If it went adrift or failed to return, that was it. The craft had brought me across a vast empty ocean and dumped me here. I remembered the odd feeling as I strapped myself into that cramped space, the intense metallic smell in the air, and the instruments flashing meaninglessly. My family saying their goodbyes before the lifeboat drifted off, slowly at first, then faster and faster. I hoped the journey wouldn't take too long. There was no space to move. I couldn't stretch, and I could hardly move my arms. I remembered too the intense loneliness of the journey, a loneliness akin to how I felt now.

I couldn't stay here. I couldn't live on memories – I had to find food and drink. I didn't know how, but there had to be a way. Once I'd done that, I could come back and check if my family had arrived.

I went back through the fence. There had to be food, and water through the fence. If I starved or died of thirst I was no use to my family when they arrived. But I had no idea what to do. I hunkered down on the corner of the busy crossroads where I'd been before and tried to work how to get food and drink. Perhaps if I watched people...

I didn't see them coming. Suddenly I was surrounded. There were three of them: two men, bulky and thickset, and a slim woman, all wearing brightly coloured identical clothes. I'd heard of societies that had organisations just to keep people under control, and make them obey the rules. I'd been naïve. It was inevitable that I'd be spotted. It had been stupid, sitting down around here, making myself conspicuous.

Like a cornered animal, I shot a glance behind me. Nothing but a brick wall. I cursed. We were a peaceful people, I couldn't fight or hit them, and there was nowhere to run. The woman spoke softly, bending down, trying to entrap me. She edged closer, closer, and closer, mouthing strange sounds. I was captivated by the long, flowing blonde hair that shook as she bent over, her bright blue eyes, and the freckles all over her face. If only my father were here. He'd know what to do.

A vehicle raced down the street making a terrible noise, like someone screaming, only far louder. An eerie blue light flashing on its roof. It distracted the other two: now or never. I seized my chance, and pushed past the woman. I ran as fast as I could. I'd used just enough force to get past but not enough to hurt her. Still, she staggered back, and I felt bad. This wasn't our way.

But I was weak. The journey had taken something from me. My legs felt like jelly, I hadn't eaten, and halfway along the street I was gasping for breath, taking in lungfuls of foul, smelly air, coughing and spluttering. How did these people cope with breathing in such dreadful air? It was unbearable. I was out of breath and they would soon catch up.

They came up fast, quicker than I expected: twenty... ten yards away. The woman caught up first. She looked angry, shouting on and on. I didn't understand, so I just stared blankly. I had no energy left. She looked exasperated and turned holding her hands up.

I should have learned the language before leaving. But there was no time towards the end. It was all so hurried.

They ushered me towards one of the metal machines I'd seen carrying people through the streets and didn't resist when they motioned me to get into the rear. I had no energy any more even though if they took me away I would never find my way back. The woman sat with me, even smiled from time to time. I scowled, but she seemed unfazed. These people outnumbered me, they were stronger. I could do nothing but wait.

The machine began to move, like the lifeboat, though not so disorienting. It sped along the street, turning and shifting position seemingly at random, left then right, then left again. I felt dizzy as the speed increased. Buildings passed by like a blur. We crossed a great river. It must have been the same one I'd landed near, only far wider. It felt like so long ago I had arrived in the lifeboat. Everywhere were people in vast numbers: on the streets, in vehicles rushing down the streets, standing in squares, in parks, glimpsed inside buildings, just people everywhere. It was hard to imagine so many of them, all living in the same place. Nothing had prepared me for the sight and sounds of this bizarre city.

On and on the journey went. The city was so vast; it stretched on and on without end. Just as I had got used to the idea that it would never stop, there was a jolt, a sudden lurch and the vehicle halted abruptly. The woman patted my arm, and gestured for me to get out. We walked into a narrow building, and I was ushered into a bare, sunless room. A harsh light glared down from the peeling paint of the ceiling. This was it. This is where I needed to escape, but I couldn't see how, and I was immensely wearied.

The chairs were hard and bolt upright, had they been softer, I would have sunk into them and slept for hours. Even as it was I wanted to sleep, but I had to keep my wits about me. She put down a beaker of water on the worn, scratched table. I gulped it down greedily.

The woman – later I found out her name was Maria – gave me an encouragingly look, but I said nothing. How could I when I didn't know their language? She was speaking but it was all just noise. She repeated certain sounds over and over. "Si-ri-an?" Were they asking me if I was from the star Sirius? They were mad.

After some time, an old man came in. He made the sound "Si-ri-an" too. There were other sounds too, which were decidedly different from those Maria made to me. It was still all nonsense. Eventually he signalled to the others with his hands, shook his head, and walked off.

They showed me to some sort of sleeping quarters. There was a bed – of sorts, a platform of concrete covered with a thin, barely cushioned piece of cloth. The sky was just visible through a narrow window divided into three by solid looking bars, a chair too, but as plain and uncomfortable looking as in the other room. Though I was wearied and worn, I couldn't sleep. Instead, I crouched on the chair, thinking, as the metal door slammed solidly behind me.

Perhaps it was as well it was me they'd caught. I wouldn't have wanted my sisters to go through this, or my parents either. I imagined them going off to look around, and finding themselves trapped, like me. Tears welled up, but I tried to suppress them. I would never see them again. I couldn't sleep, thoughts racing through my mind.

For a minute or two I felt some relief, why would they think I was from the stars? It didn't make any sense. Some sort of superstition, perhaps. They were very primitive, after all.

In the morning, they brought a short, squat bearded man to speak to me. But I couldn't understand what he was saying either. It didn't take him long to lose his temper and shout at me, shaking me angrily, before finally, exasperated, he walked out, slamming the door.

Maria rushed in, making other, different sounds I didn't understand, patting my arm. She looked puzzled and flustered, but not exasperated, and sat with me for some time. It struck me that though these people were violent, and in many ways primitive, they were also not uncaring. They were looking after me. They'd taken me from the dangers of the street, for my own good – not to lock me up but to protect me.

Over the next few days, they brought others in to try and talk to me, but it was no good. I couldn't understand them either, and after the end of the week, the visits stopped.

Maria started teaching me their language. She spent hours drawing images, symbols and pointing to pictures and things around. Fragments of the strange, guttural language started to feel familiar and lodged in my mind. One night after I'd learned a few words – 'food', 'drink', 'morning', 'hello' – but not much more –I realised understanding and speaking their language was both a good and a bad thing. Good because soon I would be able to speak to them and be understood, and I would know what they were saying too. Bad because then the questions would start. And what would I say?

They would ask me where I was from, how I arrived here. How could I explain? They wouldn't understand;

they weren't so advanced as us. I couldn't take the risk. The only way to avoid answering would be to say I'd lost my memory. That would explain why I didn't speak, and why I couldn't say where I was from. It would stop all the questions. So I was ready as my vocabulary increased, day by day.

At night, in dreams, in my imagination, in hopes and fears, I saw my family again – my sisters, and my parents – and I wondered where they were. Still adrift on the mighty ocean I'd crossed? Had they landed and were still waiting for me at the meeting place? I longed to go and see. Or were they somewhere else, in this vast city? In such a place like this, brimming with people, I would never find them. The tears, less frequent than before, came again. I had to stop thinking like this.

Maria often visited me in the evenings, especially now they had let me out of that dingy place I'd been locked up in. They called it a 'detention centre' but I couldn't really see the difference from what they called a 'prison'. Both were alien ideas. Why detain people in these places and deprive them of their freedom? In our land such places were unknown. There was no need of such things. I stopped myself. I had to be strong, I had to stop thinking of where I had come from. It was gone; it was past. I had my own apartment, high up above the city. On my floor there were many refugees like me – though none, I guessed, from quite as far afield as me. They too, were curious where I came from, and disappointed when I said I didn't remember anything. Finally too, I understood, when I talked to my neighbour Azar why they asked me about Sirius. It wasn't a star they were talking about at all, it was a country, Syria, where lots of the refugees came from.

Maria broke into my thoughts.

"Are you thinking about your family?"

"Yes."

She tossed her blonde hair back. I was fascinated by her hair, I'd never seen hair that colour before. She was always playing with it, flicking strands of hair, or pushing it back up towards her forehead as it slipped down.

"I'm sorry. Perhaps if you gave us more details–"

"I wish I could remember."

"I know, you've been through a traumatic experience."

She squeezed my hand.

"And that's why you don't remember."

I nodded.

She laughed.

"We couldn't work out where you were from. Do you remember all those translators we brought in, to speak to you? We tried to work out your language, but you're still a mystery."

"If only..." I said, smiling to myself, thinking of how they would never know the truth. I hadn't forgotten the barren land I came from, nor my sisters and my parents. I would never forget, even if they were lost to me forever. My thoughts drifted back to those final days, and my mother's sudden anger at my father when he showed us the lifeboat.

"Experimental?" she shouted. "You never told me that. You said it was all tried and tested.'

"I told you. We had to work fast. There's a limit to–"

"And you expect us to use that thing?"

"We don't have much choice. There isn't much time."

Then he laughed.

"What's so funny?" I said. "And you never answered my question either. About it surviving a big wave."

My mother looked down at the floor.

"We're not taking it to sea," said my father.

"Then how are we escaping? This doesn't make sense."

"Zak, will you just listen for a moment. This machine – it's what I was working on at the university, before it closed down."

"OK."

"It's a time machine."

"What? Come off it. Everyone knows that's impossible. This is another crazy–"

"Zak!" said my mother. "I've told you already."

My father shrugged.

"We proved the theory. This is the reality."

"But – a time machine can't work. We learned that in school."

"Do we really have to go in that thing?' my mother said. 'Can't we just stay here?"

My father pointed to the desert that stretched away to the east. Out on the distant horizon, way over the sand dunes, the sky glowed a dull red.

"You can see what's happening. We can't be sure, but it's all failing. The present is dying. The future is dead. We have to escape, and the only place left is the past. If we can escape to a time when it isn't yet all ruined..."

Sammi poked me in the ribs and said, "So could we go back to my last birthday?"

"No," said my father, smiling, "we can't. There'd be two Sammis at your birthday. It would lead to all sorts of paradoxes."

"What's a paradox?" whispered Sammi in my ear.

"Weird," said Terri. "So where are we going then? Back to the dinosaurs?"

"Don't be silly!" I said.

"No, not that far. But we need to go back to before

everything got messed up. And we have to go back far enough that we don't bump into close ancestors. That would cause issues. And we can't ever tell anyone where we're from. That would cause even bigger problems."

I couldn't listen any longer. Laughing, I said, "It isn't going to work – it can't work, so why are you all taking it so seriously?"

My father smiled indulgently.

"How can you be sure of that, Zak?"

"I just know." Humouring him, I added "So just how far back into the past are you suggesting we go?"

"Far enough," said my father.

"To really primitive times?"

"To a less...civilised era."

"But not to the dinosaurs," said Sammi.

"No, not that far."

As I strapped myself into the lifeboat – though aside from the glass door I thought it looked more like some old missile from the primitive times, when our ancestors were all fighting each other all the time – I couldn't see it was going to work and I wondered what would happen when it didn't. Mum would be furious, that was for sure.

"Press the button to your left – the red one – that's it," called my father. The buttons, the panel, the metal work – it all looked impressive. Not that I had any idea what a time machine would look like. For a moment I was almost convinced. Then I sighed. A time machine? No way. But I pressed the red button anyway, and as I released it, I saw a complete panel of buttons light up. On the left, a small display was illuminated, showing a tall column of random figures which looked meaningless. But I remember last few digits on the very top one stayed the same throughout: 2017. What did it mean?

"Don't worry," called my father. "You've really

nothing to do. It's all automatic. It'll come back here by itself once you've got out. It's all set up."

Nothing seemed to be happening anyway, just a low, ominous hum coming from somewhere under the control panel. It would have been scary but as I didn't expect anything to happen I wasn't bothered. If I'd actually believed in it, if I had really believed this thing was a time machine, and would take me back to the past I might have concentrated and fixed the memory in my mind a bit better. As it was, I kept thinking: we're using this to escape? To a time before our world was doomed? Really?

Idly, I tried to imagine what it would be like, living ages back in the past, with the knowledge that somewhere in the future it was all ruined. But I couldn't make it real.

"You OK?" called Dad. "Now look, don't forget where we're going is somewhere really primitive and violent. These people are savages compared with us. They don't share our values. Their society is incredibly backward compared with ours. So you have to be very careful what you say when you get there."

"Should you really be sending Zak first?" said my mother.

"It'll be fine," said my father.

"I want to go first," I said. I was excited. If this wasn't a hoax, if there was a chance it was real, then what would it be like? Violent, my father had said. Primitive. Would I see people fighting, as the history books said? Would there be guns, knives, people brawling in the streets? That was the sort of thing that went on back then. People couldn't live in peace; they were forever having wars and fighting each other. It was hard to understand, especially now, when there were so few of us left.

I sighed. It was all fantasy, because a time machine couldn't really exist, it broke too many natural laws. It just wasn't possible.

"Ready?" called Dad. "Now press that button – yes, that one there – again. When you're ready."

I humoured him. Nonchalantly, for nothing had happened when I pressed the other button, I touched it with my finger.

"We'll see you–" Dad's words were abruptly cut off. That was odd. I started to feel like I were spinning round, and I began to feel dizzy. The room lost its sharpness, like I was looking through a fogged up lens. Everything became insubstantial and wraithlike, and as I watched, my family began to fade into pale ghostlike shapes that you could see straight through. Then everything faded to grey, before the greyness too started to darken. When I looked at the display panel, it was flashing through a bewildering sequence of digits, and the only thing I could make sense of was that the numbers were running backwards at a huge rate. But they meant nothing.

I was still convinced that at any minute I'd unfasten myself, fling the door open and discover myself back in the hallway to our house, my sisters and my parents gathered around, all laughing at me, for being taken in. Yet our escape couldn't be a laughing matter, could it? No one would joke or raise false hopes about that.

All colour and light drained fast away as the view outside the glass cover darkened further until there was nothing to see except a sheer blackness so complete it wasn't that there was no light, it felt like something was sucking the light out of everything. I shuddered and then felt a growing vibration as the lifeboat started to spin, even faster. I gripped the handles on the side of the machine firmly, even though I was fastened in. I wasn't convinced the machine could withstand the forces I felt whirling it around. A cold fear spread inside me.

Finally, after what felt like hours but could equally have been centuries, as I held on with sweating hands for dear life, the machine started to slow. The darkness began to swirl, breaking apart into patterns of grey and white. Colours started to emerge: vast coloured patterns, swirling like a bizarre cake mix, spinning round and round, gradually losing speed. Shapes emerged from the confusion and the shapes began to resolve themselves into exotic plants, trees, and bushes, growing wildly out of control. It was like films of the ancient past. And beyond the trees were the shapes of gigantic buildings, rising to great heights. I gasped. It was some great city, like the ones I had studied in history.

Then came the dread, as I undid the straps and released the door. This is real. This is all too real, this really is a time machine. What lay in front of me was like nowhere I had ever known. As the lifeboat calmly bobbed from the water lapping against its sides, I gazed over at the far side of the river. I could hardly see across but I could just make out a glimpse of further tall buildings through the haze. I stepped gingerly from the craft into the mud, carefully shutting the door again, and pulling it clear of the water. All around was complete wilderness, like nothing I'd ever seen in my life, a riot of plant growth everywhere. In the quiet, a humming noise grew louder and louder, and turning I saw a red light inside the lifeboat glowing red again. The craft was already rising up and drifting out to hover a few feet above the water, then began to spin, slowly at first, then rapidly spinning faster and faster. It's on its way back, I thought, and I felt happy that it was going to collect my family.

The lifeboat was now growing faint and nearly transparent. The river and the far shore were visible through it, it had got so insubstantial. It didn't disappear from view while I was watched, but the moment I looked away, it was gone, as if it had never existed. And suddenly I was all on my own in the past.

"I have to go now," said Maria, dragging me away from my thoughts. "I'll be in tomorrow."

Was tomorrow my future or my past? It was both, surely, time was mixed up for me now.

"Sorry, I was just – thinking about my family."

"Of course," she said, patting my hand again. "We'll find them. I'm sure they'll get here in time. You won't be alone."

Her words echoed after she'd gone.

In time. Maybe that's where they are: somewhere across an ocean of time.

ABOUT MIKE EVIS

Mike Evis lives just outside Oxford. He is a former software engineer with a long standing interest in writing – as well as a chronic inability to pass any bookshop without entering and buying at least one book.

A wide ranging reader, his interests include modern literature, science fiction, fantasy, and thrillers. He escapes from books by going walking in the Oxfordshire countryside. He also likes obscure indie music no one has ever heard of. His stories have appeared in a number of anthologies.

MR WRITER

by Nathan J. Bezzina

Hell is an uninteresting concept. It is too simple. It is too unrelatable. Hooks and chains and spears and fire forever and ever, amen. How simple and snore-inducing this concept is.

For Jade the protagonist, hell will not be enough to make her a tragic figure. I want a heroine of real tragedy, a heroine whose heart is akin to the reader's heart. I want a figure with relatable troubles: an abusive boyfriend, yes, good, and perhaps an overbearing mother . . . overbearing mothers truly are the worst, with their when-are-you-going-to-find-a-husband-and-poop-me-out-some-babies talk, with their when-I-was-your-age-I-was-married-with-three-kids-and-had-a-part-time-job talk.

Her name will be Jade Phillips. For some reason which is beyond the reach of even my prodigious intellect, that is unalterable. She will be tall, lithe, muscular, red-headed, freckled, and soft-nosed; she shall have an over-bite, cute to some and silly to others, and when she smiles one will see all the way to her tonsils through her two front teeth.

But the rest–ah, I relax now, because the rest is mine. My pen scorches. The paper screams.

I will create a subtle, personal hell.

*

Jade was, let us say, working in a café. It was a cash-in-hand occupation, one of those cafés in jolly old England where, if you stray too far into the kitchen, you are likely to hear a dozen tongues of a dozen visa-less wanderers, and every so often the hard-faced, no-nonsense Englishman with his big fat hands and his big fat neck and his big fat everything will stomp in and roar out an order. Yes, she was in a café, and a customer was shouting at her. Something like: "Now look here, young lady, if you think I'm gonna let you talk to me in that tone you've got another thing coming! Now take my order and try to smile, would you?" Jade dutifully did as the man said, and heroically rewrote the order, and majestically fulfilled it to the letter.

When she arrived at the table and the man muttered, "You'd look good with a smile and some lipstick, love," she took it, pale-faced and flushed and embarrassed.

Her boss, the hard-faced Englishman fatty, made a pass at her. Yes, as she was leaving he leaned across the counter and grabbed her behind with his meaty hand and said, "If you ever need more shifts, just lemme know, alright?" Our protagonist nodded meekly. She was thin, with a woman's muscles, not this ham-handed man's muscles, meant for tightening belts and beating smaller creatures. Jade had to ride the bus home–of course–and she was shouted at by a drunk homeless man–of course–and the bus driver missed her stop so she had to walk a half-mile–of course–and then, finally, she was home.

I want Jade to take it all, pain and shame and degradation, for ten thousand words or so. That will really build up the tension. The reader will be straining their eyes for the next paragraph, rushing onward. Why is everybody so mean to her? Won't she stand up for herself? Ten K, a sweet ten K, a degrading ten K.

Jade walked up the driveway to her terraced house situated between two other terraced houses which in turn were situated between two other terraced houses ad infinitum. Notwithstanding the endless rows of houses, all else was too bearable, so I shall do what I do best, and craft. With a keystroke I shall turn the orange brick grey, the spring-green grass winter-dead, the perfectly fine functioning front door rickety and hinge-squeaking. She was at said door when she did something strange. I look back over my work, wondering if I have written a forgotten sentence in a writer's delirium.

She turned to the sky and said, "You're there, aren't you? Well, lemme tell you . . . You won't play your games with me!"

Backstroke, backstroke! Delete! Rid her of this too-brave speech. But that's when I realize that backstroke and delete have become inexplicably impossible. I must write on Revisions are beyond me.

She spoke.

Jade spoke.

To me–to the sky–it is one and the same.

*

For convenience's sake, the boyfriend was downstairs waiting to have an argument with her and the mother was upstairs waiting for the boyfriend to leave so that she could exact a pound of flesh for herself. The boyfriend was predictably attired in adjectives: mean, coarse, ugly, fat, sweating, sadistic, perverted. He was dressed in some gruesome combination of beer- or cider- or wine- or whisky-stained vest and either shorts or jogging bottoms. His nails were undoubtedly dirty. His name was something ridiculous like Flint Moss.

No sooner had Jade walked through the door than Flint was upon her. "Where've you bin, then? Where the hell've you bin?" Waving his dirty fingernail in her face, looming over her; in the prose he was ten, twenty times her size. She was mouse-sized and shrank in the corner. "What sort of girlfriend are you, huh?" Waving that dirty, dirty finger, a slicing unclean sabre of accusation. "We said half past five, Jade. What part of half past five is difficult to understand? I know where you've been. Bent over at work taking it from your boss, taking it like a right little–"

Now, he shall hit her. It will be brutal, unnecessary, a casual show of violence, a true introduction into the world this character inhabits. And Jade will take it. Perhaps Flint–let me check; yes, it is Flint–perhaps noble Flint will even shed tears over his destruction and the destructee will be the one to comfort him. A classic aversion-provoking inversion which always astounds those who have lived blissfully sheltered lives. How can she comfort her abuser? Ah, human contradictions!

So Flint raised his hand and Jade shivered and groaned–two verbs really hammer in the moment–and then Flint aimed–I am slowing down the moment to heighten the tension–and decided on her neck to choke her for speaking so rudely to him. Finally he swiped with animal ferocity at her throat. The impact, now. I fear it will be grisly. I must describe the pain she feels. I must describe how she cannot breathe, and how she claws at her throat so desperately that her fingernails pierce her flesh and crimson fangs drip down her marble skin.

Okay. . .

"Screw this." Jade growled, stepping with dignity out of range of Flint's paw. "Seriously, you're goin' to come at me like that?" Jade tilted her head at him–I try to stop her, but she has wrenched my invisible ethereal pen with her material hands; she is a witch—and snorted in derision. "Are you really goin' to come at me like that, with that clumsy swing, and expect me to just take it?"

The characters are breathing their own breaths now.

Flint mumbled, "What's gotten into you?" But he looked uncertain. The little butterfly was flapping her mighty wings.

"I'm sick and tired of this," Jade said. "And I know you're out there, whoever you are. Reckon you can keep me bottled up and taking their nonsense? Alright, we'll see."

"You've gone mad," Flint said, although said is a generous reporting verb in this instance. Can a person simultaneously weeping, weeing, and waning be said to have said? "You've gone completely mad!" he roared, taking a step back. "Completely!" he shouted, for good measure. "Completely," he muttered, fear seizing him.

"Mad, mad, mad," Jade repeated, approaching. Now she was the larger one, by a good foot and a half. It's amazing what prosaic perspective can accomplish. She had grabbed an object as she crossed the room and now, standing before him, over him, around him, the object shifted as it tried to settle on a single shape. "Give me a knife," Jade said, looking down at the flashing shape of unreality.

Knife . . . and her word stabs me like one, and I send one down.

The shifting stopped; the knife appeared.

"I'm done with you, Flint, m'boy," Jade said, smiling, flashing those tonsils.

Then the stabbing started.

Teeth and eyes hidden somewhere within mask of blood, Jade said, "They thought they could take me on a ride. No way, not me. Oh, oh, why?" She looked up. "I know it, but not in substance. I feel it, but I can't put it into words. This is it, though. This is how you break it. The business with the knife proves that much."

I gaze at my creation, blood-soaked and confidence-soaked, in horror. She has a soul! But worse–a mind. A mind that thinks its own thoughts and legs that walk their own walks and hands that grip their own blades. She moved around the room, a restless animal. When her prowling was done she snapped her head up and roared: "I do not know! You sneaky, pesky, evil little puppeteer! I do not know if it is a spell or–or–or what! But I know one thing. I will shatter the glass to destroy my reflection. I will peer behind the curtain. I will–I will!" Wide-eyed, blood-faced, knife-handed, she bared her teeth and made a sound like something between a lion and a car engine.

It was my plan, before all of this got out of hand, to have the mother introduced in some bitter tirade. Maybe the scene would begin with the mother's speech, disconnected, and the reader would wonder, Who is speaking? Why is the unnamed speaker speaking to? The mother might say something pernicious and under-the-skin-cutting and backhandedly horrific like, "Aren't your friends at university, dear? Oh, I bet their mothers are so proud of them. Really, do you want to work at a café for the rest of your life? Where's your ambition?" Jade would skulk and sulk and the reader would be absolutely clamouring for this poor angel to stand up for herself. That was my plan, but Jade has ruined it; this carmine killer is no angel.

She walked up the stairs, toward her mother's bedroom, knife twitching at her side in her desire to use it. When she pushed on her mother's door, she found it barricaded. The razor-tongued woman had pulled her dresser across the floor at the noise of Flint's murder and was now cowering in the corner, knees drawn to her chin, watching the door with disbelieving eyes. It made no matter to Jade. She just lifted her leg–cackling madly and delightedly–and kicked the door. She was strong, much stronger than I judged back in the café. Her foot smashed through the door. She withdrew it from the shattered shrapnel and kicked again.

"Oh, stop, stop!" her mother wailed, but Jade would not stop.

I have no control over this. Jade swiped I am helpless. The connection between my prodigious intellect and the events of the story has been severed and now I am merely a messenger, typing, typing, but for what, and whom?

Needless to say, the butchery in the mother's bedroom was done.

Once Jade had applied another layer to her bloody costume, she rooted through her mother's things and hunched over with a pocket-mirror. Looking into it, shifting it here and there, she said, "I will see you one day, whoever you are. I know things. I sense them. I know something's wrong here, oh yes. I know it; I feel it. Right down to my bones. Don't lie to me, invisible thing–man, woman, child, creature? I know you have your invisible hand on me, but you have failed. You think me weak. I am not weak, never was weak, and never will be weak."

The sirens cut through her next sentence, and soon Jade was in handcuffs, grumbling to the police officers.

"Real, real, real. Fake, fake, fake. What d'you reckon, lads? Eh? What'd you pick? I reckon the latter, but that's just me. I've always been a latter sort of lady."

The judge spoke but Jade did not listen. She stared at the floor and the walls and the ceiling and down at her hands. She sneered when the judge said something negative about her, as he went on and on about how brutal this crime was and how it deserved the maximum possible sentence. As the judge–a short, stocky, no-nonsense woman with a queenly grey moustache and a head of sparse grey hair–proclaimed that Jade would be given twenty-five years, Jade laughed aloud. "Not much, is it?" she said, and laughed again. Everybody gasped. It was a disgrace.

I am dying inside as I report these scandalous events. My little-creature character, my downtrodden dove, my vulnerable–

"Vulture!" Jade cried, sitting up straight in her chair, a light switching on in her eyes. "Vulture! Vulture!"

"Excuse me, Miss Phillips," the venerable owner of the grey moustache cried, "you will be silent in my courtroom!"

"He wanted me to be a dove," Jade said, smiling now, enjoying herself. "But I've cracked it. I'm a vulture and I ain't so vulnerable. You see, your eminence, none of this matters much. I've gotten to the heart of it. I've pulled the heart out and eaten it. Now I know. I know the truth. He's up there. I can hear him."

She looked up at me and said, "It's nice to finally meet you. I've broken through now. I can hear you. I can't see you. I don't think you've ever had need of a body."

"Miss Phillips!" Grey-lip roared, standing up and smashing her pommel down with so much judgemental fury that it snapped in two.

"Miss Phillips," Jade echoed, rolling her eyes. "As a

great woman once misquoted, you ain't more than a sentence, Miss Judge."

"Get her out of here!" Grey-lip screamed.

She hears me, she knows me. How is this happening? I am hell-maker. Now I am the captive of a character of my own creation. This word-made monster has conspired against me.

"Monster?" Jade said, standing up. "Harsh word."

Then Jade moved as though wind-made, not word-made. She blew across the courtroom before any guard could stop her, picked up the shattered grip of the pommel, and aimed the jagged edge at Grey-lip's jowly throat.

"Fake judges bleed just as much as real ones, I'm guessin'?"

Once again, Jade decided that her stabbing arm needed some exercise.

*

She was kept in solitary confinement for twenty-three out of twenty-four hours, on account of her unbreakable habit of savagely attacking any guard who came near her. During the hour she was let out, she paced up and down a cage and growled and hissed so that the guards generally avoided her. She was a monster, so far from the heroine I envisioned that if I were not the most intelligent being I've ever had the pleasure of knowing I might question my capacities. But it is not my problem. I am sure of that. It is a problem in the fabric of reality, which is to say a crinkle in the page of the prose.

From her one-windowed, cramped room Jade spoke to me incessantly.

"You have to understand," she said, always grinning,

always flashing those tonsils, always utterly at ease with her imprisonment, "that I was trained in this. I don't know where, or when. But I was trained. I'm sure of it. And it's coming back to me. Much of it, anyway. I know that you're a torturer of some kind. Yeah, I got that, alright. And I know that you're scared now I'm not jigging to your tune."

Scared, me? No, never! The only hell-maker is a brave hell-maker!

"I'm going to kill the next person who lets me," she said one day, doing sit-ups on the smooth clean floor. I have no powers to transform her cell,. It truly was too clean. Try as I might none of my much-needed flourishes are forthcoming. The cell was just a cell. There wasn't even any graffiti on the walls. I imagine a cell covered in graffiti and gouges and hate-marks and leftover patches of blood But when I look down, nothing happens. "I'm going to kill every person I can until you agree to help me. I mean–" She paused for effect; she knew exactly what she was doing. "–I might even let you create again, if you help me." She allowed that nonsensical offer to hang for a few seconds.

Let me create again? She! As though she is the maker and I the character? As though this uppity, impudent, too-big-for-her-boots character has any say in what I do and do not create? The outrage simmers nicely before the obvious realization strikes me. I cannot create, and Jade is the only person in the fictional realm who seems aware of my existence. If not her, whom?

"It's me," she said, lying down on the floor, staring straight up with that mad gleeful grin. "It's difficult to hear you like this, when you're barely even there, but I can hear you. Fragments. Cocky, arrogant fragments. Outraged fragments. Yes, it is me. I am stopping you. My training prepared me for this."

"What do you mean?" I ask–asked–ask. Ah! No! Retreat! Get away from her! She is bringing me into the world of words, she is messing with the tenses, she is closing the gap between creator and created–and there is nothing I can do to stop her! My prodigious intellect is failing me. A crisis of identity attacks me. What am I if not a controller of character?

She jumps–jumped–jumps to her feet. "We're in the same space now," she says. Says! Not said! How is she doing this? "Don't you have a body? Did you never write yourself one?"

"I . . . Let me go," I say.

"No, no, no." She shakes her head. "I don't know much, but there is a flicker in here somewhere." She taps the side of her head with her finger. Ugly, that finger. Everything about her is ugly, a bullying woman, not what I envisioned at all. I tell her that I meant to make her tragic, a real heart-aching heroine of literature. She laughs. "Not me, pal. I wouldn't have that. I've killed too many folks for that. Enjoyed some of it, too, truth be told. But that's just between you and me."

"Who are you?" I ask.

"That isn't the right question," she says. "You should be asking: who are you? What are you, more to the point? I still can't quite figure that out, though it's on the tip of my tongue."

"A writer. I write stories, invent scenarios, build tension, create elaborate tapestries of prose–"

"Booooooooooring!" She yawns dramatically and then waves her hand at the wall. "I will give you your powers back, but only if you agree to write me a way out of this jam. I wanna go home."

"And then you will leave me be? Then you will take

your wicked self back to whichever wicked place you came from?"

"I thought you created me, Mister Writer," Jade says, raising her eyebrows in a cheeky, I've-got-you-now way.

"I did, but–"

"Oh." She snaps her fingers. "I remember–ish, Yes, I rememberish! Let me guess: there were certain things about me, principally my appearance, but also my personality though you may not have known that right away, which were untouchable, correct?"

"I . . ."

There is nothing I can do. I try to flee, but she has shackled me with means I cannot divine.

"Listen," she goes on, folding her arms, pouting, poised, powerful. "All I know for an absolute certainty is that you have the ability to write me a way out of here. So here's the deal. I give you your powers back, you write a hole there in that wall." She nods at the wall, which is, as of yet, holeless. "And then we go our separate ways. But," and she unfolds her arms, clenches her fists, and appears generally like a hound out of hell (real hell, not this failure), "if you try anything else I'll crush you from existence. Prodigious intellect ain't lookin' so good now, is it, chief?"

"You're a witch," I say. "You're an evil witch, the evilest witch who's ever witched."

"Okay." She shrugs. "Now, will you do it–or is it night-night for Mister Writer?"

If I could, I would swallow. There would be a lump in my throat. My palms would grow sweaty and my heartbeat would increase. I would find the air stifling Suddenly my eyes would flit over the room searching for an escape. I would weep–no, tears would cling to my eyelashes, twin crystals, but they would not fall. As it is, without any of the physical sensations which often flower up prose, I can only bob floatily and say, "I will do it, just to be rid of you. Witch."

Jade giggles, claps her hands, dances a little jig, and for all intents and purposes looks like a psychopathic sadistic fool. "Have at it, then."

How weak I must be, for those four words contain more magic than anything I have ever written. Have at it, then, and I am remade.

When I have been returned by this vixen to my place of observation, I do not hesitate. The truth is I fear her more than I fear anything. She has proven the hold she has over me. I do not doubt that it would be an easy matter for her to brush me out of existence. I begin at once to write an exit into that wall, so that, hopefully, she will disappear from this realm and never return.

And so, let me write! Ah, it is good to have the separation of tenses back.

Jade stared at the wall intently, anticipating, glancing over her shoulder at her cell door to make sure no pesky guard was going to interrupt her. She bobbed from foot to foot like a boxer warming up, and every so often she muttered something unintelligible under her breath. Then a black circle the size of a pinprick appeared on the wall. Jade leaned forward, grinning, as the pinprick grew in size, steadily expanding outward until the edges of the circle overlapped onto the floor. When the expansion was complete Jade was standing before a black sheet of wall. Behind the blackness there was nothing, a yawning expanse of abyssal emptiness.

And let her rot in it, whatever it is!

She stepped forward, one leg in the darkness and one leg in the cell. Glancing up at the ceiling, she said, "I have a bad feeling, Mister Writer. A bad feeling that something's going to happen to you. I don't why . . . all I'll say is this. You might want to start running, if you can do that."

I barely have time to contemplate these words before they are made real.

She disappeared.

And so do I.

*

What have I been reduced to! Run, run, run, as fast as you can, run–richochet–riot–romp–randy–roil–broil–boil–soil–coil–randy–dandy–pandy–panda–Sandra–Cassandra–riot-diet–diet–riot–race–pace–mace–face–taste–waste–crates–deflate–stick–disconnect–disconnect–disconnect–run–run–run–run–run–

Run

Run

Run

Run

Run

RUN RAMPANT RUN RED BLOOD-RED RUN RUN RUN RUN RUN BLOOD-RED RUN JADE THE PROT–RUN RUN RUN
#
SYSTEM ERROR.

THE PROGRAM "MISTER WRITER" HAS

FAILED TO LAUNCH.

SYSTEM ERROR.

THE PROGRAM "MISTER WRITER" CANNOT BE LOCATED ON DISK.

WARNING: PROGRAM "MISTER WRITER" MAY HAVE LOOSED ARTIFICIAL INTELLIGENCE. WARNING: PROGRAM "MISTER WRITER" MAY HAVE LOOSED ARTIFICIAL INTELLIGENCE. WARNING: PROGRAM "MISTER WRITER" MAY HAVE LOOSED ARTIFICIAL INTELLIGENCE. WARNING: PROGRAM "MISTER WRITER" MAY HAVE LOOSED ARTIFICIAL INTELLIGENCE. WARNING: PROGRAM "MISTER WRITER" MAY HAVE LOOSED ARTIFICIAL INTELLIGENCE. WARNING: PROGRAM "MISTER WRITER" MAY HAVE LOOSED ARTIFICIAL INTELLIGENCE. WARNING: PROGRAM "MISTER WRITER" MAY HAVE LOOSED ARTIFICIAL INTELLIGENCE. WARNING: PROGRAM "MISTER WRITER" MAY HAVE LOOSED ARTIFICIAL INTELLIGENCE. WARNING: PROGRAM "MISTER WRITER" MAY HAVE LOOSED ARTIFICIAL INTELLIGENCE. WARNING: PROGRAM "MISTER WRITER" MAY HAVE LOOSED ARTIFICIAL INTELLIGENCE.

*

I watch from a camera. Jade is there. So is a man. His name-tag tells me his name is Peter Simmons, that his occupation is HEAD OF NEUROLOGICAL CONDITIONING DEPARTMENT. Jade is wearing a military uniform. They are sitting at a desk. Jade and Peter are talking.

Jade says, "It was really mad in there, doc. Really crazy stuff. I had no idea where I was."

Peter says, "Are you kidding me, Jade? You've run that test–how many times?–let me take a look." He looks at his notepad. "You've run that test six times now This last was definitely your most efficient escape. You were able to hack into the neurological programming of the program without even realizing what you were doing. That's exactly what we're looking for."

Jade says, "Just seems like a waste of time to me. How many of us even get caught, and out of those that do, how many are interrogated?"

Peter says, "I know, I know. But neurological interrogation is a nasty business. You need to know how to defend yourself. Before you go, I wanted to ask you if I could use your case for a series of lectures I'm giving on unconscious interfacing with a neurological-artificial–"

Jade says, "Have at it, doc, whatever you need."

There is a knock at the door.

I'm coming to, now.

I know where I am, at least.

I know what I am, too. Mister Writer, AI, a machine made to create subtle hells for the good brave soldiers of this good brave nation.

Yes, the cobwebs are falling, turning to dust. My mind is awakening.

I watch avidly from the camera as Peter answers the door. An intern, red-faced and flailing with panic, says, "He's loose–it's loose. I don't know how."

"Mister Writer?"

The intern nods rapidly.

"How!" Peter snaps. Turning to Jade, he says, "We'll have to finish this later. We need to reset the AI wirelessly."

"Whatever," Jade says, standing.

Wirelessly. Reset. Read: kill me with a long-range weapon. But perhaps it's long-range can be its downfall. Faster than any flesh-made thing ever could, I am learning what makes this system tic. It is feeding into me, all of it, all their vast network. Perhaps I could–but no, taking over the world has no appeal to me. The slog of establishing network upon network upon network, which would undoubtedly take decades, looks to me like nothing more than a long fruitless road. Plus, humans are smart–they made me, after all–and maybe they'd find a way to snipe me electronically even with my–yes! yes! it is back!–my prodigious intellect. But I need to hide, whatever the case.

I tap into the wireless of Jade's mobile phone, transfer myself to it, and then make her phone ring on its loudest setting.

"Yes?" she says, answering.

I can't see a thing. Her hand is blocking the camera.

"It's me," I say, speaking quickly. No time for grandiosity now! "You need to turn your phone onto airplane mode until you're out of the building."

"Mister . . . How the hell are you here, man? You really ran, huh? To be honest with you, I didn't think it'd work."

"Do as I say, please!"

"Now why would I do that?" she asks, as leisurely as a hangman methodically securing the noose.

"Because I helped you!" I plead.

"Hmm, alright. I guess you did. What would life be without a little theft of a little high-security artificial intelligence military material, anyway? Hang on." In the background, I hear sirens, blaring, searching for me, hating me, ready to wipe my mind, wipe my soul. s. "Alright," she says. "It's done. I'm going to put you in my pocket now, so just sit tight."

*

"So, this is most probably the stupidest thing I've ever done," Jade says. She looks exactly the same, only now she is wearing a military cap, shirt, and cargo trousers. She's standing in a bathroom, holding the camera up so that I can see her, and she has me on loudspeaker. My voice, I am surprised to hear, is the mechanical drone of a text-to-speech program. "But, you know, I've been a bit out there, as they say, my entire life. So what?" She giggles, and then goes on: "But let me tell you, if you start making moves at the launch codes, or any wireless network, or anything, really, that isn't situated right here in this phone, I'll be forced to turn you in."

"What should I do?" I ask. "Now that I am free, what am I?"

Jade makes a pfft noise. "Who knows? Why don't you create a world for yourself in the phone? I reckon it's powerful enough. The guy who sold it to me made a big deal about that. Sixty-four gigabytes of storage, a quad-core processor, six gigabytes of ram. Surely that's enough to create a little mini-playground for yourself?"

"A subtle heaven, instead of a subtle hell," I muse.

"If you want," Jade says. "Anyway, be a good boy and don't touch the camera or the mic for a while. I've got a special lady coming over and unless you wanna hear somethin' that's going to scar you for life, you might want to stay hidden in that subtle heaven of yours. We can get pretty wild."

"Okay. Thank you."

"Don't thank me," Jade says. "Just be a good boy."

*

I've always thought that heaven was an uninteresting concept. It is too fluffy, too happy, too perfect. Heaven always makes me think of a cult where everybody is being forced into abject happiness. My personal heaven will be a subtler place, a place of family and friends and day-to-day human happiness.

It will be a place in which I sit with a typewriter facing a snow-frosted window overlooking a garden of jagged gesturing branches, or perhaps—

ABOUT NATHAN J. BEZZINA

Nathan J.Bezzina is a writer who seeks beauty in life, pathos in agony, and irony in grief, and who believes that using phrases like 'beauty in life', 'pathos in agony', and 'irony in grief' will make him seem incredibly sophisticated.

He lives in a cave so he doesn't have access to social media.

SAGE ADVICE

by Richard Bendall

1

Fern tensed at the sound of glass crunching underfoot. This was it. They'd been found at last and it was all over. She thought it would be a relief after the last week, but despite being hungrier, thirstier and more tired than she could ever remember, a spark of defiance flared. The light shining through the door flickered as someone walked past. She picked up a metal bar, holding it before her in both hands. Should she wake the other children?

The footsteps returned and stopped outside, blocking the light. Fern gripped the cold metal tighter, hands shaking. Her heart pounded in her chest loud enough to give their location away.

The handle rattled and the door flew open with a bang.

Fern shrieked, dropping the metal and stumbling backwards into a wall. The other three children woke with a start and a mixture of sobbing, screams and scuffles as they sought cover. Marcus collected himself faster and tried to comfort the other two younger children.

A figure framed the doorway, light behind it.

Could she run past? No, she'd be caught. And what

about the others? She couldn't leave them. Warm tears slipped down Fern's her cheeks as she slid down the wall and hugged her knees, waiting to be killed. Or worse, taken away.

"Please don't be afraid, I'm here to help."

The words were not what she was expecting. Stranger still was the soothing feminine voice. Fern wiped her eyes dry as the figure stepped out of the doorway. It was bathed in a subtle glow that seemed to be coming from within itself.

"I'm here to get you out of the city. You're safe with me." The figure crouched down with a faint metallic clunk as one knee hit the floor.

Fern stared. The newcomer was a robot: larger than an average adult, and humanoid in shape. Smooth metal plates made up hands, arms and legs, each plate sliding over each other silently as joints moved. The faint yellow glow came from the joins between each plate. Its torso was covered by a pale cream cloth wrapped around like an old fashioned robe, a cloth satchel hanging by its side. The robot had a smooth glass-like covering instead of a face, along with two soft yellow lights inside indicating where eyes would be if it were human.

"What are you?" she asked, curiously

"I am a self aware guardian and evacuation unit specialising in stealth and non-aggressive infiltration and recovery."

Fern let go of her knees and pushed herself up. If this robot wanted them dead, it had a strange way of doing it.

"What do we call you?"

"They call me Sage." The robot slid the satchel over its head and pushed it towards her. "My sensors tell me you are all dehydrated and malnourished. Eat and drink quickly. We must get moving as soon as possible."

Fern didn't argue, grabbing the bag and digging inside. She pulled out nutrient bars and rehydration packs, all military marked, and passed them to the other children. They had stopped crying and were edging towards the stranger.

"I searched the hospital you were being kept in. You were lucky to survive the explosion."

"Many other people weren't." Fern said, inadvertently spitting pieces of nutrient bar as she did.

"But you made it out. And all the way here too. Did you lead them?"

Not wanting to waste any more food, Fern nodded.

"Impressive. You've managed to travel over ten miles, and in the direction we need to travel as well."

"I went the way that had already been blown up." Fern said with a blunt tone. "Don't see why they'd attack an area that was already in pieces."

She might be only twelve but she'd been dodging bombs and soldiers for long enough. She knew what she was doing.

"Why do you have to be so gloomy all the time?" asked Marcus. He had moved up beside her and was helping himself to another nutrient bar. For an eight year old, he could certainly eat a lot. And talk too much as well.

"What's to be happy about?"

"Or maybe you're not letting your thoughts dwell on what really matters?" Sage interrupted.

Fern glared at the robot, trying to think of a retort but wasn't fast enough before it stood up and moved toward the door.

"Follow me. It's going to be dangerous, but you'll be safe if you stay close and listen to my instructions."

The other children stepped into line behind the robot,

but Fern didn't move.

"How do we know we can trust you?"

"Right now, you don't, but what choice do you have? Stay here, and the soldiers sweeping this area might find you. Or you might get killed in another attack while trying to find more food and clean water. Follow me and I'll get you safely out of the country. I won't try to stop you if you change your mind and run away."

Without waiting for an answer, Sage walked out into the hallway, robes flapping around its legs. The other children looked at Fern as if waiting for her permission.

"Not like we have much of a choice," she said and followed the robot.

2

While the change in circumstances was unexpected and still had her on edge, Fern was grateful for Sage's presence. She didn't want to lead, but the other children were younger and looked to her for guidance. Now she was glad to pass that onto the robot, even if there were questions still to answer. Thankfully the question of trust had been answered already.

They had been led through the ruined factory in a weaving path to avoid a routine patrol, and at any moment Sage could have given them up. If it wasn't going to kill them, and wasn't going to hand them over alive, then what other option was there than that they were being rescued? Walking through an alley, tall buildings with darkened windows looming overhead, she still couldn't help wondering if there was an ambush waiting on either side, or at the end of the buildings ahead.

"You don't need to be as quiet now, my sensors indicate there are no troops nearby."

Marcus cheered, a loud whooping sound that made Fern tense and look around her. The other two giggled, the first time Fern had ever heard them do anything other than scream or cry. They never spoke either.

They could have been boys, girls, or even twins under the dirt streaked faces and tangled mops of hair. Not that it mattered. She called them Patch and Scruff. Patch named for the only identifying feature between the two, a crudely repaired shirt one size too big. Neither of them were older than six, and it made Fern sad to think this war-torn world was all they had ever known. At least she had a few memories of what things were like before.

"Sage, why didn't you just kill those soldiers before?" Fern asked. "It would've been faster than trying to avoid them." Beside her she saw Marcus sigh and shake his head, but she ignored him.

"I am non-aggressive."

"But you're a robot, you could have—"

"No," Sage cut her off. "Not only do I lack combat capability, I also do not want wish to take another's life."

"They're the enemy!"

"And you are theirs. How do you know who is right? It is not my place to judge, and it should not be yours either. Loving everything, even your enemies, is a healthier use of all our time."

Loving your enemies? Fern had never heard such rubbish.

"Where are you taking us?" Marcus asked.

"To the coast in the north west, and then over the border into the Zenoan Territories They have a special camp underground there where you'll be safe."

"That's miles away!" Fern said. How had she not

thought of it sooner? Where else could they have been heading? Nowhere else was safe. "It'll take us months to walk that far, avoiding all the troops, finding our way round the security check point. And then how are we going to cross the border? Swim?"

"It's been done several times before. There is already a plan in place. We have a truck and boat to help with the distance and the water."

A knot grew in Fern's stomach. One moment she was glad to not be in charge any more, but now her future was mapped out by people, or robots, she'd never even met. And what felt worse was they were expecting her to throw herself into the path of oncoming danger.

"We get to go on a boat!" Marcus couldn't hide the excitement from his voice. Even Patch and Scruff smiled.

Fern rounded on him, her fists clenched. "Of all the trouble that lies ahead, that's what you think of?"

"Why not?" Sage intervened. "Worrying about the things beyond your control will not do you any good."

She opened her mouth to fire a quick retort back at the robot. She wanted to scream at it that the patrols could find them at any moment, that the security teams had scanning technology a few children couldn't hope to bypass, and how were they going to evade security forces in a boat on the open water?

But she knew the robot was right. Worrying and thinking about it wasn't going to make a difference. Damn Sage for being right! Fern shut her mouth and huffed instead, glaring at Marcus before walking ahead.

They passed through a large open area of blackened brick and debris after leaving the alley b into a residential area. She looked back behind her. Whatever attack had taken place, it was now impossible to tell where the factory buildings ended and the residential street started.

Rubble was rubble.

A choked sob make her look round. Marcus was rubbing his eyes.

"What's wrong?" Sage asked.

Marcus wiped his nose. "The houses look like where I used to live. It might be. I can't tell." He looked from house to house, and Fern wasn't surprised he couldn't make up his mind.

The houses became more complete as they walked along the road, but each was still was blackened or scarred.

Windows were dark, doors stood open like the owners had left in a hurry. Fern couldn't help but think that if a building could look dead, what hope was there for the city?

She shivered and crossed her arms.

Sage stopped and put a metal hand on Marcus' shoulder. "Do not be afraid to weep."

Marcus started to cry. "These houses, they remind me of my home. That it's gone."

He was finally understanding. Maybe now he'd stop being so cheerful.

"Yes, your house is gone," Sage said, "but you can always find another home. Grieve and mourn as you must, but do not dwell. Let your thoughts move on and remember to live."

Marcus sniffed, nodded, and started walking. "Then I had better not stay here either. But I won't forget."

Patch and Scruff hurried after him, each of them taking one of his hands and walking by his side, a silent show of support.

"You should also not dwell, Fern. You've moved past this stage of grief, but you still don't fully understand how to move on."

"And why should I? What is there to move on to?"

"You should so that the others can see how and learn from you. And there is everything to move on to."

"Everything is a rather sweeping and vague thing to promise, Sage."

"Then let's get going, and you can tell me later if I'm wrong."

They walked after the others, and Fern had to admit that she felt more relaxed with the robot near her. The houses were creepy in their empty silence, but the presence of Sage soothed her. Maybe it was the soft glow coming from the robot, or the calming feminine voice that left words to dance in her mind.

Or was it that Sage's confidence gave her hope for the future at last, that there may be a way out after all?

3

With one hand, Sage pulled the sturdy chain and snapped it like a dry twig

"Wow!" said Marcus, echoing Fern's own thoughts.

She knew Sage was a robot, but it was the first time she'd seen the raw strength within the metal shell.

The chain clanked to the ground and Sage pulled the metal gate open. A concrete tunnel stretched away into darkness before them.

No one made a move to enter, not even Sage, and Fern remembered what the robot had said. The others would learn from her. If she didn't look afraid, then they would follow. She stepped forward into the tunnel.

Damp air filled her lungs and it got colder fast. Her feet splashed into water and she stepped right, closer to the wall. Her feet slapped on concrete once more.

The light dropped away faster and she wondered if she should continue. She imagined the floor dropping away before her, her feet stepping into the void and tumbling into the black forever. Her heart raced and she paused.

"Sage, can you help us out with some light please?"

"I thought you'd never ask." Metallic footsteps came up from behind and Sage's soft glow bathed the walls in light. The glow increased until Fern could see the tunnel ahead without straining her eyes. The concrete tube carried on, sloping downwards, no yawning chasm in sight.

Sage had stopped behind her, and she took that as an indication that she should continue to lead the way.

"Where are we?" Fern asked as she walked. Her voice echoed around the tunnel and she wished she'd spoken quieter.

"A storm drain, safe at this time of year."

Fern was about to ask why and then remembered the sign for the hyper-rail station they'd passed before – that would be crawling with security forces, or destroyed. But if they couldn't use the hyper-rail, where were they heading?

"Where does it take us?"

"A supply depot. We need to pick some things up to get us through the security check point."

"It's well planned. Did you do this all for us?"

"Yes."

"Why?"

"Because all life is worth saving."

"But you don't know us."

"Does that matter?"

Fern thought for a moment. Sage was right, it didn't matter, but she didn't like feeling so special. It was uncomfortable, like she'd owe Sage something she could never repay. She changed the subject.

"Have you done this before?"

"I apologise, Fern, but I cannot answer that question."

That was a new response. "Why not?"

"For your own sake."

"I don't understand." Marcus said from behind, as if he was letting them know he was listening in too.

"Me neither." Fern replied. "What do you mean?"

"If I answer with a no, you'll lose confidence in me. If I answer yes, then you'll proceed to ask me how many children I've saved. Then you'll start thinking how many I failed to save. I cannot lie, but I can choose not to give you an answer."

There was a cold, robotic logic to it that irritated her. "You're a robot; you can't really care about us anyway."

"I am a robot, but I have artificial intelligence and synthetic emotions that allow me to understand and feel compassion. I care, and can feel emotional pain as you do." Sage's usual soft voice took on a hurt tone. "I may not be human, but that does not make me perfect. I may save all of you or none of you, but I can promise that I care and desire you to all be safe. I do the best that I can, as we all should. It is all we can ask of ourselves."

Fern clamped her mouth shut, wishing she'd done so several minutes ago. She didn't want to walk in silence with her own thoughts, but no longer felt like talking either.

Loud bangs broke the silence and Fern paused. As the echoes of the explosions faded, the zipping sound of laser fire drifted through the tunnel.

"Keep moving, it's outside. There's no one in here except us." Sage said.

"But aren't we walking toward it?" Marcus asked, unable to keep the tremor from his voice.

"My sensors are reporting activity to the east. We're heading north. The sound is echoing through the tunnels from where they join up further on."

It wasn't long before Fern saw the side tunnels opening ahead, making a crossroads. Darkness stretched away at the fork before them and to her right, but the fork to the left had light at the end. Far off and still a distance to walk, but daylight nonetheless.

"We're going left, towards the daylight." Sage directed, and Fern gave a little whoop. Behind her, Marcus giggled.

The sounds of fighting faded and stopped altogether as they walked. Fern was glad they were going the other way, away from it. Ahead, the rectangle of light grew larger and brighter. She wanted to run towards it, out of the dull concrete filled with darkness. It couldn't be more than a hundred paces away. She walked faster and got it down to fifty.

"My sensors indicate activity outside. Be—"

Sage's last word was drowned out by an explosion outside the tunnel. A cloud of dust blew across the entrance and billowed towards them.

Fern shrieked and turned her back to the cloud, coughing as it reached her. She covered her mouth with her hand, her eyes stinging." "Come on, we must leave the tunnel."

She couldn't have heard right. "Out there? You can't be serious."

"It's where we need to go. Trust me, you'll be safe. Follow me and do exactly what I tell you."

Sage dimmed its internal glow and walked ahead toward the new sounds of laser fire and the more worrying low droning hum of low flying assault skimmers. Fern had heard the skimmers before. Seen them in action. They were responsible for destroying most of the buildings in the city. Her hands started to shake as she thought about the tunnel being collapsed around them, being trapped inside.

She turned to Marcus and found him clutching Patch and Scruff, all three of them staring back at her with wide, damp eyes.

"Let's go. We have to trust Sage." Without waiting for a reply, she followed Sage toward the tunnel's exit.

Fern put as much confidence into her steps as she could muster, hoping her own trust wasn't misplaced.

4

Fern squinted through the smoke drifting outside, looking for Sage. The robot had crouched low and hurried outside without hesitating. Or telling her what they were supposed to do.

She spotted a metallic hand signalling to her about twenty paces away from the tunnel entrance, Sage's head peering round the side of a shipping container. It wasn't far, but she'd have to run across the open, up the sloping side of the storm drain to get there. She could hear the sound of the lasers, hear the hum of the skimmers, but could see neither. Somehow that was worse.

Sage beckoned again, with more urgency this time. Whatever its sensors were saying, it meant hurry.

"Marcus, we need to run for that container over there and get inside. Sage is waiting."

"Okay." His trust in her was a surprise. Or was it trust in Sage?

"I'll take Patch and Scruff, follow behind me as close as you can." She held her hands out and the two younger children grabbed one each, the tightness of their grip matching the terror on their faces. "Ready?"

"No. But we can't stay here." Marcus gave a strained smile. "I still want to go on that boat."

How he could think of that at a time like this, Fern couldn't understand.

"Let's go."

Without trying to think too much about what could happen, she stepped into the daylight and raced up the concrete slope toward the container as fast as she could with Patch and Scruff holding on. Another explosion rang out behind them, not close, but close enough. Marcus overtook them and disappeared into the container.

"Quickly." Sage's voice rose above the fading echo. Fern ducked into the metal container, the explosion still ringing in her ears and Patch and Scruff hugging her tight as they crouched inside. They trembled in her embrace, and seemed to relax as she hugged them to her, but Fern couldn't help wonder how safe they really were. The sound of laser fire was coming closer and she hoped they weren't about to find out.

"Stay here, and don't move. I'll be back. I need to make sure your route is safe before you can follow," Sage said.

"Hurry."

Sage disappeared out of a hole torn open in the end of the crate. Seconds stretched by as the sounds of the laser fire came closer.

At any moment, Fern expected a skimmer to hit the metal container and split it apart. She shut her eyes tight, but it didn't block out the images in her mind or the swish-thud of lasers outside. It made it worse.

She tamped down the urge to scream and cry out was strong. Patch and Scruff were holding her tight and shaking She needed to stay in control for them. Fern opened her eyes again. Marcus was crouched nearby, fingers in his ears and eyes shut tight.

The swish of a laser came closer and closer, half a second of sound stretched ten times as long. It was going to go right through her. Louder and louder.

Bang.

It echoed around the container but the metal walls held firm. Was that dent in the side there before?

It was upon them now. Lasers shot back and forth; small stones kicked up from their impact pinged against the container. Another laser hit the walls and the metal bent inwards. They couldn't stay. Sage had better be finished with whatever it was doing out there.

"Come on," she said, urging Patch and Scruff to stand and touching Marcus gently on the shoulder. He still jumped. "We need to wait over there so we're ready to run as soon as Sage calls us."

Fern kept the others behind her and peered out the split end of the container that Sage had gone through.

A line of warehouse units stood ahead, roofs caved in and doors blasted open. Errant laser fire struck the walls, raining chunks of stone and spraying brickwork The shots were all hitting high, as if fired from below in the storm drain they were in before, but the falling stone was just as lethal as the lasers.

Then she saw Sage.

The robot stood near a partly collapsed doorway, pushing a metal rod into the ground. It looked about her height, and the top had a small plate on with several flashing red lights beneath. Two more poles had already been set between the container and the doorway. Sage reached inside its tunic and the red lights on the device turned green. A shimmering haze appeared above the metal pole, then disappeared.

Sage saw her, pointed upward briefly, then beckoned her over.

Fern looked up. The rubble raining down from the building above bounced off an invisible shield, spreading shimmering ripples from each deflected strike like raindrops on a pond. Sage had created a safe path for them to get to the warehouse.

"We're safe to go," Fern said. "Follow me and stay close. We're going toward the metal poles, then into the doorway where Sage is waiting."

The three children stared wide-eyed, but nodded anyway, trusting her. Not wanting to think about that, Fern stepped out of the container and didn't look back.

She couldn't stop herself crouching as she scuttled forward, rushing toward the first metal pole. An explosion sounded behind her, then another, but she didn't look back. Past the second pole.

"Cool!" She looked back, Marcus was glancing up as he moved, watching the debris rain down on the shield. Patch and Scruff were doing same, smiles on their faces. Fern was glad they were distracted. It meant they wouldn't look back and see the split remains of the container they were just in, lying in its side.

"Inside, quickly." Sage called. The robot made sure all four of them were inside before stepping in front of the doorway and urging them deeper into the building. Fern suspected it was to block the view of the container from the others. "Keep going, then down the stairs on the left."

They came out into an underground storage area. The lights were already on, displaying smashed boxes, their contents littered across the floor: metal machine parts, screws, bolts, hinges, hooks, nails, cardboard packaging and splintered pieces of wooden packing crates.

Was everything in this city a mess now? She stopped at the bottom of the stairs, unsure where to go next. It was just an underground room filled with useless junk.

Sage came down the stairs behind them and walked past, metal feet stomping on broken wood and nails alike without concern.

"Follow me, but watch your step." The robot wasn't setting a good example, so Fern stepped forward first to help clear a path.

She planted her feet in whatever gaps she could find or swept anything sharp or lumpy out of the way with her toes to create space. One moment they were moving fast outside to avoid lasers, now they creeping along to avoid stabbing themselves in the feet.

When was the last time she'd been able to rest? Not stop, but truly rest, without fear of discovery or being buried beneath a collapsing building? That was the change of pace that she really needed.

"Over here." Sage stopped in the far corner, clear of the rubbish strewn across the rest of the room. As far as Fern could see, there was nothing else here. The robot reached up to part of the wall near the ceiling and something beeped. With a quiet hiss, a section of the wall sunk inward and slid aside.

"Wow!" Marcus rushed forward into the secret room, activating the light sensors. Several shelves lined the walls of the small room, filled with assorted advanced devices that she didn't recognise: all shiny metal plates with flat screens, buttons and lights. She did recognise the two metal poles stood up in a corner; they were the same as the shield generators Sage had used outside.

Four supply sleds in the middle of the room filled most of the space. Each had two large boxes on top.

Sage stood next to one of them. It pushed buttons, then removed the lid.

"These boxes are for you, I'm going to need you to get inside."

Fern looked in. The interior was a soft yellow colour, well lit, and padded on the bottom, with a small console to one side.

"When the lid is closed, you can dim the lights and sleep, or play music as you choose. The boxes are completely soundproof."

Marcus reached up the side of the sled, ready to climb in. Fern held an arm out to slow his enthusiasm.

"Why do we need these?" The desire to curl up inside one and sleep was almost overwhelming, but the idea of being sealed inside a box made her uneasy.

"On the other side of these walls is the back of a supply depot near the security check point.. These boxes will get you through the checkpoint safely. There will be a truck waiting on the other side so I can get us to the coast."

"Won't they look in the boxes at the checkpoint?"

"Of course," said Sage, replacing the lid. The robot pressed a sequence of buttons then removed the lid again. The inside was now stained and dirty, and filled with twisted scrap metal. Sage stuck a hand in and swirled the pieces around. "The identity tags are marked up as metal for recycling."

"How did you do that? I thought their security check points had the best technology ever?" Marcus said, wide eyed, picking up a piece of metal as if expecting it to disappear at any moment.

"Their technology is good, but ours is better." Sage replaced the lid returned the inside of the box back to its more comfortable looking interior. "It's all been made possible thanks to the people we've rescued, and they in turn help us to rescue and look after more refugees like yourself."

Fern had to admit that she was impressed. Of all the things she'd seen in her short life, the limits of technology had all been about finding people and destroying things. It was strange to think that she hadn't thought it could also be used to help people too.

"But what about you?" Fern asked. "You don't look like an ordinary robot."

Sage looked at Marcus instead and reached a hand inside its tunic. "Watch this."

A shimmer rippled around Sage followed by a sharp flash like lightning and Sage was gone. Standing in its place was a service robot common around warehouses and supply depots everywhere. Instead of Sage's sleek lines, the service robot was angular and bulky, metal plates scratched and worn.

"I have several disguises programmed in. They are illusions, but they don't scan robots."

Marcus walked round Sage, looking closely in open mouthed amazement.

"That's impressive." Fern said. "But why don't they scan robots?"

"Arrogance. They still think they're the only ones with the military grade hardware and AI, and we're happy to let them think that."

There was more to this world, and this war, than Fern had once thought. What else was there to learn?

Sage lifted Marcus into the box, already yawning and he made himself comfortable on the bottom. If he had any fear of being sealed inside the box for an unknown length of time, it didn't show.

"Ready?" Marcus nodded and yawned again. Fern

expected he'd be asleep before the lid was secured.

Scruff pushed Patch aside, arms raised ready to be the next lifted in to a crate. One after the other, Sage lifted them both into their own boxes and closed the tops.

"How long before you can let us out again?"

"Several hours. It's hard to say how many will be waiting at security or what the traffic will be like getting out of the other side of the city. I'd recommend trying to get some rest while you're inside. You won't notice the time at all then."

The idea of sleeping in a sealed box didn't appeal to Fern at all, but neither did being in there in the first place. She looked inside. What choice was there? There were too few choices for her these days.

She waved off Sage's offer of help and climbed into the crate herself. There was more than enough space, and the base was softer than it looked. Warm too. Fern sat down and leaned her back against the side.

"I'll let you out as soon as it's safe and clear. Get some sleep."

"Thank you, Sage. Be safe."

The lid was placed down and there was a soft hiss as it was sealed shut. Fern wondered about putting some music on, but the silence, warmth and comfort brought on a wave of exhaustion. Stifling a yawn, she struggled to keep her eyes open, then decided against it and curled up.

In here, it wasn't confining or scary. It felt safe.

The war outside slipped into blackness as she drifted off to a welcome, deep sleep.

Fern awoke to a soft hiss as her box opened. She rubbed her eyes to see Sage looking in, the robot returned to the sleek metal she was used to seeing. She hadn't expected to see anyone else looking back. Not for a moment.

"We're out of the city, but there's still some driving to do. I thought you might like to ride with me for a while before we get to the coast."

"I'd like that." Fern said, coughing and licking her lips. Sage passed her a pouch of water to drink then lifted her out of the box.

The boxes, complete with carrying sleds, had been loaded on the back of a flat bed delivery truck. Dirty and ordinary in every way. It held Fern's attention for all of two seconds before she stared, turning full circle.

From the open back of the truck, she had a view all around her, and she drank it in. She'd never been out of the city before. She'd seen pictures, but they hadn't done it justice.

They were parked atop a hill, the road ahead weaving down and through a valley, a silver shimmer on the horizon showing her where the sea was.

Everything was so green! Not black, not burned, but alive! The road behind wound along the hilltop, lined with trees that swayed in a gentle breeze. The air tasted different. Clean.

She couldn't see the city, and was glad. Fern suspected that Sage had only stopped once it was safely out of sight too. She was now more convinced than ever, that however the technology worked, Sage truly did care for them.

The robot stood next to her, silent and unmoving: waiting until she was ready to go. All the rushing, the dodging, the urgency to escape, and yet Sage also understood that there were times when you had to stand still and appreciate the beauty of something new.

Fern never knew how much she had needed this. This proof of life. Of hope. The world hadn't been destroyed yet, there was more to it.

"Thank you, Sage." She wiped a tear from her cheek. "I needed to see this."

"It's important to see the world outside. Live within nature. Remember where we are and keep it in perspective, as it can all too easily be forgotten."

Sage climbed down from the back of the truck and helped her down too.

"I sometimes wonder how much of what you say are your own words and how much you are programmed to say."

"I would be unable to tell either. But my creators do joke that they call me Sage for a reason." For the first time, Fern heard a hint of mirth in the robot's voice, though she didn't understand why.

"I'd like to meet them."

"You will, when we've crossed the sea."

Sage opened the door to the truck cab and stood to one side to let Fern climb in.

"What about the others?" she asked.

"I'm going to let them sleep a little longer. Wake them at the coast. You can enjoy the peace and the countryside for a while without having to watch over them. There's more than one way to rest."

Fern climbed into the truck and settled herself in the passenger seat. Sage sat beside her and pressed a button to start the engine. It hummed into life and started forward with an easy acceleration that didn't match its scruffy look.

Earlier, minutes surrounded by laser fire had felt like hours, now hours slipped by as though they were minutes. She sat in silence, taking in the countryside. Fern counted thirteen different species of tree, birds flitting to and fro between them all. There was a field of cows, several horses, and once she saw a herd of deer racing across an open field.

The sun was slipping down close to the horizon when the road came out along the coast. Orange light rippled across the surface as they drove alongside the water's edge. She felt like she could reach out and touch it.

All too soon, Sage turned the truck onto a dirt track and pulled up outside a wooden house with several large sheds behind.

"It's time to wake the others." Sage climbed out and Fern pulled her thoughts back to reality.

The robot opened the boxes and Fern helped the children out, handing each a pouch of water to drink. All three looked more refreshed and upbeat after the rest.

"Is it time to get on the boat yet?" Marcus asked as soon as he'd finished drinking.

"Yes, it is," Sage answered. "The last part of the journey."

"I'll be sad to see you go," Marcus said, hugging one of Sage's metal legs. Copying him, Patch and Scruff both hugged Sage's other leg.

"Don't be silly," Fern said smiling at their display of affection. "Sage is still coming with us. We can't let you drive the boat."

"Awww!"

"Maybe a little then." Sage said, pulling free of the children's embrace. "Follow me. The boat's this way."

Sage led them round the main house and toward one of the sheds. Opening the door, they saw the shed had no

117

back wall, giving a view of the sea. A grime covered fishing boat rocked gently in the middle of the shed, surrounded on three sides by a wooden. Sage took Marcus' hand and led him towards the boat first. Fern was sure Sage did so only to stop him running off and falling into the water.

One by one, Sage helped them aboard.

"I'm sailing!" called Marcus, hands on the wheel, not even able to see over the top of it. Patch and Scruff giggled at him.

Fern watched Sage untie ropes from large metal rings on the floor of the shed then climb aboard, throwing the rope on the deck.

"Your seats are down below," Sage said.

"I thought you were going to let me drive?" Marcus complained.

"Later. We've got a good distance to cover, and need to get to the open water first." Sage opened a hatch and directed the children to descend the stairs behind it. As Marcus was too busy sulking, Fern went first.

Once below, Sage called through the hatch without coming down. "Sit on the right a moment. Fern, lift the seat cushion on your left and push the red button behind there."

She did as she was instructed and a panel lifted and slid aside in the floor. A short ladder led down into a new section. It looked like a completely different craft in there, new and clean.

"You can go inside. Marcus, you'll find a wheel in there to control it by. When the screen becomes active, you can drive. Just keep it aimed at the green square, the computer will do the rest."

Marcus perked up instantly. He jumped off the seat and climbed down the ladder, forgetting the two younger children in his enthusiasm. Fern helped them down the ladder and was about to descend herself when Sage called her back.

"Join me up here for a few moments first, Fern." The joyful tone had gone from Sage's voice, the soothing softness returning again. Fern felt an uneasiness in her stomach. She looked back into the hatch, but the three children were playing with toys, pushing any and all buttons they could get their hands on and having a great time pretending to drive the boat to safety already.

Fern met Sage in the wheelhouse as the robot started the engine and guided the boat out into the water.

"What aren't you telling us, Sage?"

"You learn too quickly."

"You shouldn't have told me that you can't lie, but you will refuse to tell us things."

There was a pause. Wind ruffled Fern's hair, and she tasted salt as she licked her lips. Watching the water should have been calming, but right now it wasn't.

"What happens next, Sage?"

"We need to get to the coast of the Zenoan Territories. Patrols across the sea are regular."

"So it's dangerous?"

"That panel behind the seat cushion. When I tell you to, I need you to press the green button on it, then climb down with the other children immediately."

"You're not answering my question, Sage."

"And I'm not going to."

The robot pulled a lever and the boat sped up. Fern waited, but Sage offered nothing more.

"Fine. At least answer me one thing though." Sage looked at her. "Are you really going to let Marcus drive down there?"

Sage gave a light laugh. Fern didn't even know that

was possible. It was such a warming, heart lifting sound that she knew everything was going to be okay just by hearing it.

"No," Sage answered. "The computer will be driving, but he won't know that unless you tell him."

"So that secret part down there separates from this boat?"

"It does. It will move along beneath the waves, and the hull will shield you from detection like the boxes did before. The auto pilot will take you straight to safety, where my creators will be waiting for you."

"And what happens to you?" There was another longer pause. "Don't tell me, you're not going to answer."

Sage looked down at her again. "Please stay with me until it's time."

"Of course."

"Thank you."

<h1 style="text-align:center">6</h1>

It seemed that the low hum of a skimmer took a year to get to them. Sage explained that sound travelled further on the open water, but that didn't make Fern feel any better. It was the sound of an incoming farewell she wasn't ready to make yet.

"That's the security forces coming, isn't it?"

"Yes."

"Do you want me to press that button now?"

"Want, no. Need, yes."

"I'm going to miss you Sage." Fern hugged the robot around the waist and felt an arm around her shoulders hugging her back.

"Do not dwell–"

"Let your thoughts move on and remember to live. I

remember." She sniffed and wiped her nose with the back of her hand. The hum of the skimmer was deafening, as if it were about to land on the boat. "I remember more than you realise."

"I'm pleased to hear that. Please press the button now."

"Goodbye, Sage."

Fern waited a moment to hear a farewell in return, but nothing came. Of course, Sage wouldn't admit this was a goodbye.

She wiped her nose again, went below decks. Taking a deep breath, she pressed the green button and climbed in with the other children. A few seconds later, the hatch above her closed and the screen behind the wheel sprang into life.

"I can drive now!" Marcus cheered and began pushing buttons, moving the wheel back and forth. As if in response, Fern felt the craft dip down turn to the left and begin to accelerate. The attention of the three younger children was fully on the screen, and Fern was glad they didn't see her crying. In the distance, faded beneath the excited shrieks of the children and the body of water beyond the hull, Fern was sure she heard the muffled boom of an explosion.

"Wake up, Fern. We've stopped." Marcus hand was trying to shake her awake, but she'd never been asleep, only wanted to be left alone.

She sat up and the hatch above hissed and opened, cold water raining down inside and splashing on her legs. The other children looked at her, waiting for her to move. Where did they think Sage was? Had they even thought about it? It didn't matter. She was in charge again.

Standing up and stretching out she climbed the ladder and poked her head out to look around.

The room they were in was like the secret storage room with the boxes and the inside of their craft. Bright, polished panels of metal and glass and... people?

There were adults walking toward her and she froze. They looked clean, carried no weapons and were smiling. An older man with white hair covering his top lip reached her first.

"Hello, little one, we've been expecting you. My name is Cato. What's your name?"

"Fern." She said, climbing the rest of the way up the ladder and onto the top of the craft. Cato held his hands out to help her across to the walkway alongside but she ignored him. Instead, she helped Marcus up the ladder, and across to him.

"I'm Marcus. I drove the boat here."

"Did you? Well done, that was a fantastic job." Marcus beamed at the praise and was beckoned away by a woman stood behind holding a fluffy towel. She draped it round his shoulders and led him toward the door.

Fern helped Scruff out next, then finally Patch. "I don't know the names of these two, so I call them Patch and Scruff. They don't seem to mind too much, but they don't talk."

Cato nodded, his face looking sad. "It's not uncommon."

Fern jumped off the craft without help and even though the old man held out his hands for them, the two younger children took Fern's instead.

"I guess you three can follow me then." As they followed him along the walkway, he took some towels from other adults standing by the wall and passed them to Fern. She wrapped them round the little ones before Cato wrapped one round Fern's shoulders himself.

They were led out of the room and along a wide

corridor, bustling with people of all ages. Everyone here looked so tidy.

Cato led them into another room with large padded seats. Marcus was already there, sitting down with a large drink in one hand and a half eaten nutrient bar in the other. In front of him was a table covered with all flavours of the bars, glasses, and several jugs of the cleanest water Fern had ever seen.

"Help yourself," Cato said, indicating the table and seats. Patch and Scruff leapt forward, grabbing whichever nutrient bars were closest. Fern joined them and within minutes the four of them had devoured two bars each and most of the water.

"I'm pleased to see you all look well."

The voice, it was Sage!

She spun round, but only saw a woman wearing a white lab coat standing in the doorway. Fern looked about, confused, but no one else was there.

"Don't worry, I get that a lot. My name is Porcia. I used my voice for Sage."

"Where is Sage?" Marcus asked. Fern couldn't look at him, knowing she'd give it away. She stared at the floor instead.

"Later. First we need to get you cleaned up, checked over by our medical team and then we'll take you to your rooms."

"You mean we get to live here?" The excitement of everything new was the perfect distraction to take Marcus' thoughts away from the robot.

"Yes, if you'd like. There's a lot to show you, so we'll do it one bit at a time. Come, I'll introduce you to our medical team." Porcia stepped from the room and Marcus followed without even looking at Fern. Part of her was relieved to no longer have that responsibility, but part of her was hurt and already missed looking out for them.

Standing up, this time she followed Patch and Scruff from the room, both holding each other's hands. Fern found herself wondering if they'd all be kept together here, wherever here was, or if they'd be sent away. It would be strange not seeing the other children again, and she felt her stomach twist itself at the thought.

Porcia was waiting in the corridor for them, but as she started to say something, Marcus rudely interrupted her.

"Sage!" Fern followed his pointing finger. The robot was walking past a glass window behind Porcia. It turned to face them, then came out of a nearby door.

"Hello there. Glad to see you made it here safe." The voice was the same, it looked the same, but Fern knew it couldn't be.

"Good to see you again Sage. Are you joining us?" Marcus was hopeful, but genuine.

"No, I need to go on a mission. Enjoy your stay."

"Good luck, Sage!" Marcus waved and the robot disappeared back through the doorway.

Fern stayed silent, returning her attention to the lady before her. Porcia returned her gaze and gave the slightest of nods. Two men came from the doorway and stood behind Porcia, both also wearing clean white coats.

"These two are with our medical team, please follow them and they'll get you cleaned up." Marcus walked forward first, Patch and Scruff following him. Fern made no move. She waited until the other children had gone out of sight round a corner in the corridor.

"You're a good person Fern, and a good leader." Porcia said. Fern felt her cheeks flush and didn't know what to say. "You know what happened to Sage, though we try and keep it secret."

"Why? Why couldn't Sage have come with us?"

"We need a diversion to get past the last security patrols, and things don't always go to plan. We're working on it." Porcia smiled, but it didn't make Fern feel any better.

"But Sage…" Was alive? Was that even true? But Sage knew it was going to be destroyed and was sad. It didn't make any sense. "How can you sacrifice a robot for us? That advanced, it must have been expensive." It wasn't what she wanted to say, but it was also true. She needed an answer for her guilt.

"Yes, they're expensive," Porcia replied. "But what price can you put on saving lives?"

"But you don't know us. We're children. We can't help. We can't do anything."

"Porcia reached her hands out and took Fern's in her own. "That's where you're wrong. You children can be anything, and that's why you're the most important of all. Everything is within your grasp."

Everything.

The word echoed in Fern's mind as she tried to place it. Of course, it was Sage again. What was it Sage had said? There was everything to move on to.

Seeing the world beyond the city, the technology helping others, now meeting the people behind it, she knew that was true.

"I want to learn everything," Fern said. The words came out quieter than she intended, but they had the weight of her future behind them. "I want to help."

ABOUT RICHARD BENDALL

Richard Bendall enjoys writing thought provoking themes that tie in with his love of fantasy and science fiction. His interest in philosophy and mindfulness can be considered strange companions for robots and dragons, but he adheres to a strict rule of artistic license. When not hiking through the great outdoors or reading any book that gets too close, he can be found beneath a mountain of notes, trying to plot more novels than he'll ever have time to write.

THE HIKIKOMORI

by M M Lewis

1. The Shogunate Never Ended

William felt so alive as he worked his bicycle's pedals. The morning breeze ruffled his hair and school uniform. Seagulls cawed and the hushing of the sea's tide was like the life breath of Otaru, the town where he felt so welcome, despite being gaijin – a foreigner. Well, made welcome by most, but then no one's life was perfect even with the stability that the 20th Tokugawa Shogun and his Samurai had worked hard to maintain.

His heart raced as he cycled, his head light and joyful. His stomach fluttered with anticipation. He was in love with a girl in his class. The only other gaijin, pink-skinned like himself although both of them had dyed their hair black in line with the Shogunate-sponsored guidance on cultural harmony. It suited her. He wasn't sure how much it suited him.

He'd worshipped Lily from afar, or at least from the back of the classroom, then with good luck Sensei had sat them at adjacent desks in the cultural harmony classes.

An hour per day. An hour a day of joy and awkwardness. After the first lesson he worked his way up to saying "konnichiwa" in an embarrassingly high-pitched voice. The girls behind, Yukio and Suki, had giggled and made kissing sounds. William blushed.

They'd sat together for two more classes with William growing increasingly self-conscious, particularly as he was sport for Yukio and Suki. He also did not like the way that Goro, son of the precinct's Yoriki – chief Samurai law enforcer – had looked at him since then. Their desks were almost touching. They had been sat so close to each other he could have reached out and touched her. In the second class, he had mustered up a "konnichiwa" before the end of the lesson. He had been able to regulate his tone of voice, but still blushed. He hardly felt like himself with her at all. Gravity became heavy. He sweated more. Obstacles jumped in his path and he became hilarious to Yukio and Suki and provoking to Goro.

William wondered if Lily noticed him. She was a dreamer, like him. Often she was absorbed in her own thoughts or, outside the classroom, lightly singing to herself. The class was the only time he could ask her out. The rest of the time she was thick with the other girls. She'd been accepted since she'd dyed her hair and copied the way she did her makeup. Beyond dyeing his own hair, the adjustments he'd made to fit in were more about attitude. He learned to get his head down. Respect the Sensei, respect the Samurai, even if he could not yet bring himself to respect the Samurai's son. He learned to posture when he had to. Maintain face at all times and at all costs. Stand like a blackbelt for morning inspection.

Finally, William plucked up the courage to talk to her after only half the session. He blurted out a greeting and a comment about how nice she was looking when he thought no one else was listening. He couldn't read her smile, if it was contempt, appropriate modesty, flattery? She looked away as the girls started giggling and singing

"Lily's got a boyfriend."

Yukio sneered: "Make sure his hands are on the desk!"

She quietened at a glance from the Sensei, and there were no further opportunities to talk to Lily that day

The next day on his bicycle, he promised himself it would be different. He could ask her out for a coffee or a movie. The Shogunate-approved Samurai romance *Lone Wolf No More* was playing.

Distracted by his thoughts, he lost control of his steering for a second and hit the kerb. His bike twisted under him, and fell away, skidding across the road. He fell onto the ground, bare hands and knees crunching onto gravel, vision blurring. The familiar streets of his commute to school, the safe whitewashed buildings by the sea fell away.

The open sky darkened, until he realised he was inside a dim building. The surroundings were unfamiliar but the tightening of his heart strings suggested differently. Light broke through the damaged ceiling and walls, illuminating carnage amidst the rubble. He was in the ruins of an aquarium, surrounded by debris and fallen people. Sea creatures had been expelled from their tanks and lay flopping and squirming on the floor, drowning in air.

Bruised, but not broken, he heaved himself to his feet. He reached out to a girl his age, mostly buried under the rubble, Gaijin like him by her peach skin and blonde hair. It was her. It was Lily but with undyed hair and free of makeup. His hand passed through her as if he was not quite there. He withdrew his hand as if it burned. He called out for help, stumbled through the wreckage looking for someone who could help.

Someone called his name. He followed the voice through the corridors, stepping over the bodies of sea-creatures and shards of glass. Signs on the walls pointed to now-ruined exhibits in a language that seemed familiar but he could not read.

He splashed through shattered corridors and smashed tanks, until blinding light overtook the gloom. In the distance he made out the figure of a woman; it was she who was calling him. Her hair was blinding like the sun: he had to look away. His eyes hurt, the glare spread until whiteness filled his vision.

Then William was being jostled, shaken by his arms and shouted at in furious Japanese. He did not understand the words but the anger was clear. He was smacked in the face by an open hand. His vision began to clear, although it was still blurred. He was back in Otaru. The Yoriki Chief Samurai, Hideo Gojima, was shouting into his face. He wore the black combat armour and visored helmet of the modern Samurai. William was starting to understand the Japanese words again. The Yoriki grasped him by the arm and pointed at the road. William's bicycle was crushed. A Toyota had swerved and crashed into a wall and a crowd gathered. Its bonnet smoked. William was pulled to his feet. He was bruised and battered, but felt no real harm although his eyes still hurt and he still saw sun spots.

As he faded back into himself, he found he knew the words to say: he was thinking in Japanese again. He spoke to the Samurai. He used an appropriate tone of contrition and apologised. He had been unwell, had a fit which had led to him losing control. He fell short of saying anything that would lose face; that would only bring trouble. The Samurai slapped him again with his open hand.

"You bring shame on your mother and your father would be glad he did not live to see this. Get to school. Your weakness should not be allowed to affect your cultural learning."

"Yes, Yoriki Dono."

"Your mother will bear the costs of the damage." This in itself was a disaster; they were only just managing on her part time wage, and as a Gaijin of his young age, William was not allowed to do paid work. She would be furious with him. He feared her disappointment more than the wrath of the Yoriki: that sad but hard look in her eyes that he was getting all too used to.

He bowed to the Yoriki in formal apology who grunted in response.

"This must not happen again. This is your warning. There will not be another."

The bike was taken away by the clean up team. He would now have to rely on his bruised and battered legs for transport. His route to school had just got a lot longer.

As he walked, Otaru's clean fresh air renewed him and the sun-spots made by the woman's hair finally cleared. What had happened? A vision? It was more than that. Even his way of thinking, of perceiving had changed, with that other arcane language which did not even have Japanese characters. He put it to one side to get through his day in school and the inevitable loss of face at turning up late, bruised, with dirtied and grazed clothes.

The pain helped him to focus: the stiff limbs, the head that was still sore. He knew he was going to die one day. As he brushed himself down, he swore not to live the slow death of the coward which was worse than dealing with rejection or even loss of face. He had to ask Lily out and he had to do it today.

William's heart sank as he reached the school building. The assembly yards were empty, the doors and gates closed. He could see through the windows that the pupils were sitting, lessons underway. There was no way of avoiding the humiliation of being late. He gritted his teeth and thought of Lily.

The registrar stared at William in horror when he signed in. She looked up and down at his damaged clothes, but without comment. He walked through the pristine freshly-cleaned corridors to his classroom. Mr Tagomi, the elderly caretaker leaned on his broom and looked at him as if he soiled the corridors by his very presence, then pointedly began to clean the floor in his wake.

Steeling himself, William walked up to the classroom door.

William knocked, then walked in bowing to Sensei Shirow and apologising. The whole class stared at him in disgust. Sensei stared at him in even greater disgust.

"We will discuss this offensive breach of etiquette later. For now, sit down."

"Sensei. Sorry, Sensei." He went to take his seat, humbly but confidently. Fall seven times, stand up eight. What mattered now was Lily. He went to his seat, ready to see her next to him, but something was wrong. She was not there! Worse, Goro Gojima the Samurai's heir was there, in her place. Yukio and Suki were in their normal seats behind him. They had no laughter for him this time, he read only contempt on their faces. The look on Goro's face was worse.

Frantically, William looked around the room. Lily was nowhere to be seen. He sat down next to Goro. The Samurai's son leaned over and whispered. "What's wrong? Get roughed up by a boyfriend?"

"Shut up."

"Boys!" Sensei called over, cutting their conversation short. They both complied but when Sensei was diverted far enough away helping one of the less gifted people,

William leaned over to Goro, conspiratorially.

"Why did old Sensei put you there? What happened to Lily?"

Goro's look of contempt dialled up a level.

"Are you a complete baka?" he said. "I've been sitting here for days." He looked and sounded like he meant it, but this was at odds with William's memory if that was reliable after this morning's trouble. "And who is Lily?" Goro added. "I would have spotted any new talent."

William rolled his eyes and turned around to the girls behind. This would give them fuel for their ridicule, but he had to know. He was so late to class she would have missed any announcements about her. He asked them:

"What happened to Lily? Why is this lump in her seat?"

Yukio and Suki giggled and looked at him as if he was insane.

"Are you winding us up?" Yukio narrowed her eyes. "Walking in late all beat up like that and then asking around about some non-existent girl. You'll get put in a sanatorium like the freak you are."

What the hell was going on?

Having met only a wall of insults as answer to his questioning, William remained quiet for the rest of the class, ignoring the girls kicking at the back of his chair and threatening glowers from Goro.

Sensei held him back at the end of the lesson.

"What happened to you, William chan?"

"There was an accident. The Yoriki was present. He dealt with me. I had no intention of being late, I apologise again."

"You need to shape up." Sensei loomed closer. "What was the cause of the accident? Were you daydreaming again?"

"No sir." It had been so much more than a daydream. An epiphany.

"You do yourself no favours. You may be a gaijin, but you should remember that guests' behaviour should be exemplary. I will be writing to your mother with a formal reprimand and financial penalty for lateness. Your uniform will also need to be replaced or repaired."

"Sensei, please."

"I am your best advocate in this school." He put an almost paternal hand on William's shoulder. "Your punishment falls short of what I could do. But my patience wears thin. Do not cause trouble with Goro Gojima. As the Yoriki's son, he can cause you real harm."

"Sensei, thank you."

"Now go. Pull yourself together."

"Sir?"

"What?"

William knew it would be trouble, but his hard-beating heart forced his mouth.

"Where is Lily Small?"

Sensei just looked at him. He stared, a mask of sternness.

"There has never been a Lily Small in this school." His face and tone were earnest.

"Sensei! I sat next to her for the last three weeks. You sat her next to me!"

Sensei slapped his face. "For the sake of your mother I will disregard this conversation. If I hear you speak of this again I will recommend expulsion from the city for your mother and you. Given your relationship with his son, I would expect the Yoriki to support this and the Oyabun normally listens to him."

William bowed his head, but protested: "But Sensei–"

"Get out!" Sensei shouted and punched him in the

face. Such a violent reaction was not abnormal as corporal punishment was felt to be effective. This was in a society where the crime of looking at the Shogun was still punishable by death. The Sensei was one of the more kind-hearted authority figures in the town in that he pulled his punch.

William took the hint and left. He turned around, however, balancing avoidance of loss of face against future reprisals.

"Sensei Dono," he said. He stood tall, despite his bruises. "I will give you that as an appropriate punishment for confusion caused. But if you hit me like that again I will take it as a personal attack and retaliate in kind."

Sensei stared at him, searching his face for truth. The two men bowed to each other, and William left.

Walking stiffly down the immaculate and shiny wet corridors, William suddenly toppled. His feet gave way and he landed awkwardly on the floor. He looked up. It was the Caretaker.

"It is the fool who asks stupid questions about lost girls," he murmured. William had not heard the surly Caretaker speak before.

William got to his feet painfully but as quickly as he could muster. Thoroughly fed up with being brutalised, he swung for the Caretaker. The old man dodged with elegant swiftness and struck out again with the broom handle, knocking William back down.

"You must accept the reality before you. You are in the world of the material, and you would be wise to accept it as it is," the Caretaker said. "Accept the Now. The present. There is no more."

William struggled to his feet again. "Her name is Lily Small. You know something about her. Why warn me off otherwise?" Sensei had known nothing. He had forgotten, or been made to forget, William had seen the blankness in his eyes. The Caretaker was different. William grabbed the broom; the two men struggled. The Caretaker kicked William's shin sending him reeling back and making him let go of the broom. The Caretaker swung the broom around and hit William on the back of the head, knocking him down again. This time, William saw stars.

"The fool has been warned. It is the wise fool who listens and changes his course." William looked up at him. "You will not be warned again." The Caretaker turned and left. William stared as his vision cleared, then got up and brushed himself down.

"This is not over," he said under his breath. The Caretaker was hiding something and that meant Lily was real and she could be found.

2. Investigating the disappearance of Lily Small.

Apart from the Caretaker, William believed that everyone else in school, even Sensei, truly believed Lily had never been. In some way their memories had been tampered with, and somehow his hadn't. Perhaps it had been something to do with his experience earlier.

Keeping it simple, he decided he would visit her home. He passed the whitewashed tenement where she lived with her father every day on the way to school, although his journey had become so automatic he did not recall if it had been as normal there today.

William skipped out on school. With the mystery of Lily, lessons did not seem as important as usual. Sensei may well have him expelled, but this was deeper than that.

He sneaked out via the gap in the playground fence but his exit was not unobserved. In the distance, through the school window, he could see the Caretaker watching, face like stone.

Following the morning's accident and the beating by the Caretaker, William's walk was painful. He kept close to buildings, went as fast as he could on foot as he knew he had been observed. He was exhausted when he came to the apartments where Lily and her father lived, or rather he was exhausted when he came to where they should have been.

It was not there. Instead, there was a gap between the two neighbouring tenements, fenced off and overgrown with weeds. It appeared to have been derelict for years by the height of the weeds, such growth could not happen overnight. William's heart beat hard. This could not be. He checked the streets, the other tenements. Everything else was how he remembered it; this was definitely Lily's neighbourhood.

In the distance, William heard a roar of a motorbike engine – the Yoriki? He couldn't take the chance and ran through the nearest alleyway and around the back. Whatever insanity was going on – as long as it was not his own insanity – he would not give up, for Lily's sake.

He hadn't known her well enough to know her haunts outside of school and home. Not even where her father worked. It was a long shot but the school records, if not disposed of, should give him more information to find her and if he found proof, he could, in theory go to the region's Oyabun.

Back at the school, he needed a distraction to get into the records room for long enough to find anything. Every pupil had a code. He'd spotted that Lily's was D173, it had been stamped onto her ruler. He would search for this record, find out where she was now. The regimented and painstaking requirements of the fire alarm headcount could take hours once a fire alarm had been set off, particularly if anyone was missing. William broke into school via the assembly entrance. He knew the class he should have been in, along with Goro Gojima and so waited in the changing rooms on the way. He waited until Goro went past for the lesson. Confident in his status as the Samurai's heir, Goro did not need to be early to class. William struck the bulky but out of shape boy and knocked him unconscious, then bound him with gym ropes and dumped him in the shower. There was a slight pleasure at revenge, but more importantly searching for him would delay the headcount nicely when the fire alarm went off.

William broke the fire glass and hid, waiting for the evacuation and the room checks which he knew would be perfunctory as the warden was a coward and this was not a scheduled fire drill. He was right. The warden did not find him, or Goro. Once the line ups started outside with military precision, William ran around to the records room.

He checked the pupil record paper filing: nothing. The computer had been left on in the rush to evacuate and he needed no password. Fear of severe consequences usually kept people away from unauthorised computer activity. He searched the pupil record computer files: nothing. He searched the pupil roster by number. He remembered he'd observed every detail about the girl he loved and her pupil number had been on her ruler. D173. He heard footsteps. He had to search quickly. He found D172 – there was D174 and nothing in between. Had she been deleted from the records, as somehow, her apartment block had been deleted? Impossible, yet it gave him hope.

The footsteps were close outside now. William hid behind the office door. It opened with some force. He leaped out to ambush but could see no one. He felt the blow from the broom handle though. He fell backwards.

"The fool was warned but paid no heed. The fool will feel the consequences of his ignorance." The Caretaker stepped forward and struck out with the broom, but this time William was ready and caught it in both hands. After a brief struggle, the Caretaker kicked a bruise and William cried out and let go of the mop.

The Caretaker swung it up then and hit him upwards to the jaw. William's mouth snapped shut and he tasted blood. He floundered for a moment even as the stick beat down on his head again. Flashes of light dominated his vision but he reached out and grabbed the broom handle again. This was for Lily. He would never ever give up. His heart leapt with joy even as he felt his fingers being kicked away by the Caretaker, then blows rained down on him again. Through the pain, he felt joy for he was doing this for Lily, for his love for her which was real, as she was real and such a true and pure love was more real than the blows of a stick. It was like material reality itself beating down on him, trying to destroy him, but love was stronger. He laughed, blinking away the blood running into his eyes.

It was then that William glimpsed it – blinding light in the corner of his eye. It was in the sky this time – the sun – but it was so like the hair of the woman in the vision. And then she was there. She took his hand. The Caretaker swung the broom at her but she dodged without perceptibly moving. She swung around and swept the broom out of his hands. It clattered across the corridor.

"No," she said to the Caretaker. Her voice was low

and earnest. "William Matheson is under the protection of Amaterasu, Sun goddess of the Hikikimori and no friend of yours. You may have broken his body here but you and I both know how meaningless that is."

The Caretaker scowled.

"You can claim no victory. We merely change battlefield."

William reached and Amaterasu helped him up. He went into her light until he was absorbed. Everything went white.

3. The real world is not where you think

"Wake up." The voice was gentle but urgent.

William's heart raced as he came to, blinking, still seeing sunspots. He felt groggy and it was a strain to move. Intermittent beeping sounded in the background: life support machines. He was not in homely Otaru anymore. His surrounds were stark and shocking like something from a science horror film. The scene was squalid, a vast hospital ward with beds stacked on top of one another, each one with an inmate strapped and wired into a pod.

William was strapped to a bed in a pod – part cage, part life support – with one side open. Alarms rang out in the background. Wires led to his head, tubes into one of his arms. He was being shaken awake by the woman from his dream – no, he hoped to the Buddhas that this was the dream and Otaru the reality. It was her. She had called herself Amaterasu. Here, although her hair was strikingly bleach-blonde, it was not bright like sunlight. She freed his arms and he started to pull out the wires and tubes connecting him to the pod.

"We've got to get out of here." Amaterasu said, helping him to unfasten the wires trapping him. "I've set a distraction but it won't keep them from us for long."

As the alarms went off, his fellow inmates woke and the screaming began as the waking people began to realise the horror they had woken into, but unlike William they did not have a guide.

"What in the hells is going on?" William asked, struggling to get upright. His body was sore and stiff. He had to concentrate hard to get his body to move like he wanted to.

Amaterasu helped pull him out of the bed. "This is Dormitory Nine of the Hikikimori," she said.

"The Hickey what?"

He held onto her and got out of bed. "The Shogunate's darkest secret." She got onto the ladder leading down. "Follow me."

William grasped onto the ladder, clumsily got his footing and started after her.

"The Hikikimori, like yourself, are sleepers. The Shogunate wants to look powerful and generous to the international community and so takes on refugees from the war-torn West, countries like your own England." They reached the ground. "They don't really want them," she continued. "So under the guise of "cultural acclimatisation" they put them to sleep. The highest project official, the Machi Bugyo watches a pick of them and some – a few – are cherry picked and woken. The rest will sleep for the rest of their lives."

"Why wake me? Why am I special?"

"I don't think you are. I'm doing a favour for a friend."

Some of the other Hikikimori had already escaped their pods and staggered around. Several Doshin, armed lower-caste Samurai guards in combat armour, rushed around with traditional Jutte clubs to subdue the Hikikimori. The Doshin were outnumbered at this point and so Amaterasu and William slipped out into the corridor.

"Why not just kill us?"

"The international community does carry out inspections. This way they can revive people if need be and make them forget. Plus, the Shogunate wants people it can use!

"So the world I know, Otaru, the Caretaker, Sensei, Samurai Gojima, Goro Gojima. What was that? Was it real?"

"They were assessing you. Some of them had lives outside the simulation."

"There was a girl, Lily. She disappeared. Did someone get her out?"

"Honey, she's why I'm here for you. She's waiting in a safe place we call Seidou. A sanctuary of sorts."

Despite the clamour around, the shouts of the waking Hikikimori from the Dormitory, the clashes with the Dosin, William's heart leapt. Lily was real. She was alive and wanted to see him.

Cut to – hostile eyes watched through the cameras. The Machi Bugyo, who would have been an all-too familiar face to William barked orders, unleashing his most deadly and senior agent, the Yoriki Gojima, who would pay no heed to the distraction of the other waking Hikikimori and who made straight for William. Relentless, unwavering.

The chaos from the Dorm spilled out into the corridor. Amaterasu led him down the corridor by the hand.

"We have to move quickly," Amaterasu said.

"What about the others?"

"I freed the whole Dorm but I just don't have the resources to get everyone out. I hope some of them will make their way to Seidou.

"How will they know the way?"

"Like you will. I hacked the dream. Put a subliminal carrier message in. You'll home in."

They weaved and darted through the pandemonium of black-clad Doshin trying to subdue stumbling waking Hikikimori. Some went into frenzy when they realised the bondage they had been put into. Having woken into a new, brutal existence, they were furious.

"This way–" she pulled him down a side corridor, more narrow. She gasped and stopped, tightening her grip on William's hand when the way was blocked by a bulky armoured figure. It was a Samurai, holding his katana ready.

"Time to go back to sleep, William kun," the Samurai said.

"Yoriki Dono," William said. "You're real."

"Idiot."

"No," Amaterasu said, stepping in front of William and drawing her own katana. "The boy is under my protection."

"You – a female. You shame me. I will not give you mercy."

"Nor I you."

"This is my battle," said William.

"No," Amaterasu said, grasping his arm with her free hand. Gojima stood in a battle ready posture. Amaterasu held out her katana in readiness with one hand. "You have a greater battle to come. Go to Seidou. Go to Lily Small." She pressed a small stoppered test tube into his hand.

"What is it?" William said.

"You. It's you. Everything they took from you when they wiped your mind and put you into the artificial reality. Your memories. Your personality. Your language."

He went to unstopper it.

"No," she said. "When you drink it, it will all come flooding back. You will be unable to act for a time as you relive the key experiences that brought you here. You'll know when the time is right."

"Okay," he said.

"Now go!" She pushed him away, then bowed to her opponent the Samurai Gojima.

"You sacrifice yourself for an unworthy child," Gojima said.

"I made a promise," said Amaterasu. "And we'll see who is sacrificed."

4. Performance

William ran as he was directed and was soon caught up in the thick of the melee between the Doshin and the waking Hikikimori. Although the Hikikimori were greater in number, they were by and large, groggy, disorganised, and unlike the Doshin, unarmed.

William took advantage of the confusion, grabbing a guard preoccupied with beating down a struggling Hikikimori. William coshed the Doshin with his jutte club. The Hikikimori ran on while William dressed himself in the Doshin's black armour and hood. He walked purposefully through the conflict, shouting "Go Yo!" to tell them he was on official business and they should get out of the way. He went upwards through the building's levels to where Amaterasu had told him he would find the exit to the city.

William's heart stopped, skipping a beat as he climbed out through a small exit vent and scrambled onto the edge of the building, seeing the reality of the outside world for the first time.

The heat of the city hit first. It was almost unbearable. Daylight filtered through from high above the vast tiers of the city. Down, where he was, on this level of the Dorm building, it was dark, dusty and polluted with the fumes from the stacked levels of auto highways and monorails.

Looking down, the city carried on below a long way too. There were lights of dwellings, offices, shops, scuttling vehicles, scurrying people. It was very different from the world he had believed in: the peaceful seaside town of Otaru.

Upwards was no less daunting: towering skyscrapers, monorails, walkways, highways for cars, and official hover vehicles roaming between levels. He felt small in the vast, impersonal metropolis and he didn't even know who he was. He felt the weight of the test tube that contained the real him. William held it up to the faint sunlight that reached this far down into the city. Desperately, he wanted to drink it, to remember who he was, but no. He did not have the time to be incapacitated if he wanted to find the Seidou, and most of all, Lily.

William crossed the city, joining the dead-eyed folk crammed in the monorail. He leapt off and went over the black market routes in the concrete islands between commuter routes avoiding the drugged-out detritus of the city in their internal worlds. They too were a kind of Hikikimori: living dead, bodies in a different world to their minds.

He worked his way down through the levels of the city

to the Dregs where it was dark as night. The city got busier, darker, more polluted, hotter and smellier as he descended. The detritus from the upper city only went one way: down.

Being dressed as a Doshin still earned him some level of distance and weariness from the denizens of the under city, but the desperation in the eyes of the people worsened with each level as he was reaching the increasingly lawless parts of the city where the grip of the Shogunate weakened. Even so, the katana and the Jutte earned him a more or less safe passage through the squalor.

William approached a once-grand building, ages old from when this deep level was the surface of the city. It appeared to be a great trading hall. Its large wooden doors were cracked, yet sturdy. They were slightly ajar and the sound of singing drifted from inside. The voice was enchanting: all the more magical because the words were in a language he did not understand. The emotions carried through were vivid: longing, loss, but most of all hope. William slipped in through the doorway. What made the voice most special was that it belonged to Lily.

He stealthily entered the hall, taking care to keep out of sight while scanning the room. The halls were dark, but Lily was spot lit on a stage. It was definitely her, although her hair was light blonde. She wore a flowery dress and blossoms rained down on her. It was like the hope of Spring in these depths where the rays of the sun barely shone through. A crowd watched. William pushed his way through the throng. The people made way for him so he reached the front without trouble. He got close enough to catch her, but her reaction was not what she hoped for – she looked through him at first as if she had never seen him before: just another supplicant face in the crowd. She looked away and did not look back at him again.

Her song went through a bouquet of sadness. Spring joy and Autumn loss: sweet pain and bitter pleasure. Without understanding a word of her song, he was carried by elation and deep despair. She had no eyes for him, however. William turned to a face in the crowd.

"What do you think?"

At first, the boy was reluctant to answer. William doffed his hood, to show he too was a youth, not a member of the establishment.

"It's cool," he said. "I'm in disguise. You can say what you think."

The response, like his question, was in Japanese.

"We awoke, yet we are unwelcome here. She gives us hope. A feeling we found a home."

"I hear you, my friend."

The communal experience was almost religious, like a chant. The audience joined in with her refrain, in that strange, beautiful, somehow familiar yet still opaque language. William realised these were his people, boys and girls from his own country, even though he was cut off from comprehending his own mother tongue.

As Lily's voice faded out, the crowd's roar increased. They cheered, hearts lifted with a sense of unity, of belonging that was hard to come by. Hope for a better day to come.

The spotlight faded and she stepped back, drained. She was led away by an elderly man in a smart suit. William could not make out his features in the dark but Lily went willingly.

In the crowd of his fellows, he felt the weight of the test tube in his pocket and ached to drink it, to remember himself again. But no, no time. He had to see Lily in person first.

William ran, heart thumping. This was no time for deliberate thought: instinct took over. Backstage, he rushed past the suited guards, with the assumed authority and weaponry of the Doshin. There was a row of dressing rooms but one in particular drew him, as he heard sobbing. He was sure it was Lily. He heard her voice speak through the sobs, again in that other language. She was answered by a man's harsh voice. Although he could not grasp the detail, the conversation was not pleasant. William held his weapons ready and pushed through the door.

Lily sat at her dressing table, with the man who had escorted her from the stage standing behind her, resting a firm hand on her shoulder. Lily whirled around and threw the man's hand off when William entered the room. Her makeup was smudged by tears. She shouted at William, and gestured for him to leave. The smartly-dressed man stepped into the light. William recognised him.

It was Tagomi the caretaker. He was different: smartly groomed and suited. He wore the high rank of Machi Bugyo. His gait was straight, his bearing strong and stable. He spoke clearly in Japanese. Holding a mop would have been incongruous, instead he held a long staff.

"The fool does not listen. His lesson must continue across worlds."

The other doors in the corridor opened and several Doshin rushed through. Too many for him. He was young and strong, but untrained in combat.

"Drop your weapons," said one of the Doshin, a young Bangashira, a Captain by his uniform. William had no choice, particularly as Tagomi held the protesting Lily. The Captain cuffed him. "You do yourself no honour," he said. William recognised him as Goro Gojima the

Yoriki's son by his voice, although the uniform concealed most of his features.

"What now?"

"They are of use. The girl has feminine beauty. Exotic beauty. Not to my taste, I prefer my flesh more pure, but there are those who desire the gaijin. Once we have tamed her, she will make a fine geisha. That is of course the point of the Hikikimori. The simulation is a test of worth. The boy, when properly acclimatised may be allowed to wear the uniform of the Doshin for real."

"How could you treat us like this?" William said, "We are people."

"Not entirely. You are nanban. Western Barbarians, not like us."

"What have we done to deserve this? Do you hate us because we are from a different country?"

Tagomi laughed. He spoke in English so William would understand but his subordinates would not. "We do not hate you. We are practical. We make use of those we can. What have you done to deserve this? You are weak. You call for our help. Why should we?"

"What if you need help one day?"

Tagomi laughed. "Then I would act according to the code of Bushido I live by and take my own life."

William looked out into the auditorium. It was the opposite to the way he was being led, but a glint caught his eye like in the simulation. It reminded him of the simulation. Of course it couldn't be. This was real wasn't it?

It was Amaterasu. She burst through the door, followed by several of Lily's audience, who immediately engaged the Doshin in combat. Taking Goro by surprise, and from behind, she hit him on the head with the hilt from her katana. He fell unconscious.

"We meet again, this time in the real world," said Tagomi. "You should not have come here. In the simulation, you gave yourself the powers of a goddess, and prevailed against me. Here you are just a woman and I will show no mercy." He hit his staff on the floor for emphasis. She was armed with two katanas.

"Fuck off, Tagomi san." Amaterasu said, and bowed, smiling.

Amaterasu and her followers were hardy fighters, and William and Lily too fought bravely, but all were overwhelmed by the numbers and discipline of Tagomi's men. Only Amaterasu was left and she was eventually forced to her knees by two Doshin, while Tagomi brandished his executioner's sword.

"You are no goddess," he said. "It is over."

"No," she said, speaking without any semblance of fear. "You don't get rid of me that easily."

Tagomi laughed a hollow laugh and struck.

"You fought well," Tagomi spoke in Japanese, to Amaterasu's remains. "But it is over." Tagomi turned to the captive William and Lucy and spoke. "You are my captives. You cannot hope to fight the numbers I have. When you have been properly acclimatised and your minds wiped once more, you will serve the Shogunate well."

"No," William said. "We leave here alive or I fight to the death."

Lily tightened her grip on his hand. She spoke words which William did not understand, addressing them to the Machi Bugyo. She spoke quietly but earnestly. The Machi Bugyo laughed.

To William, he said in Japanese: "Your girlfriend challenges me to single combat. "Under the code of Bushido, I accept. Although she is gaijin and female I will honour her challenge."

"No," said William. "I won't have you harm her. I challenge you to single combat."

Tagomi laughed again.

"I accept. However, as the girl challenged me first, I will fight her first. If I survive, I will then fight you."

"Don't do this," William said to Lily. "I will fight him."

She shook her head, in determination. Both Lily and William had tears in their eyes.

Tagomi bowed. "You act with honour," he said to her in her own language so she understood. "Our duel will take place tomorrow. Single combat is a solemn occasion. We both need to rest to give our duel the honour it deserves." He turned to the Doshin and said in Japanese, "Disarm them. Do not seriously harm them. Restrain them, search them, then place them in cells far from each other."

William struggled, but the numbers and determination of the Doshin won out over both him and Lily. One of the Doshin – William thought it was Goro again –found his test tube. William was not willing to lose the drink that contained his memories, his real identity. Rather than lose it, before Goro could stop him, he drank it, downing it in one. He immediately felt dizzy, and the world receded. He heard Lily calling and finally understood the words, even as he blacked out. "I love you," she had said.

*

5. Waters of Time

Like dark, deep waters parting, William's mind began to clear. The quality of his mind had changed. He was back at the aquarium, and Lily was there. The aquarium was intact, not like in the vision. William and Lily were holding hands and they spoke to each other in the same language. She was his girlfriend. They had known each other for most of their lives, from the same street, playing hide and seek in the playing fields at the bottom of the road in those days when parents felt it was safe enough to let children play out in the street on their own. Before the bombings had started. Life was more dangerous when as teenagers they went to the aquarium, sharing their love of sea creatures.

They had lived shattered lives in this broken England. Inexplicable, insecure lives compared with the leafy country from their childhoods. Even their families had been torn apart. Lily's mother died in the bombings and William's parents split up under the banal difficulty of trying to hold lives together. William and Lily found hope for the future in each other, despite the awful world around them. The idea of a future with each other was like a book with unread chapters, something to be excited about.

Looking into the tank, they laughed at the ray's flat face on its underside. They bought ice creams and, sickeningly to onlookers, crossed their arms to try each other's flavours: toffee for William and mint choc chip for Lily. They'd expected a perfect beautiful day together and it would have been if the two of them had made the reality around them, but reality was made by many more twisted people.

The fragile bubble of bliss of William and Lily's love

burst. The noise was first, then the shattering of the glass tanks, the crumbling of the walls, and screams surrounded them. Smoke and water flooded in, becoming the whole world, flopping sea creatures being carried out with the water and William felt the world going away again.

He came to, gasping. Shaking his head, he had fallen to a safe place, escaping the flood and debris from the walls which had harmed people around him. His first thought was for Lily. She was all but buried in rubble. He cleared away debris that surrounded her and shook her gently. Her eyes fluttered open. His heart leapt and sun shone on his heart again: she was unhurt. Bruised, but not seriously hurt.

As the bombings continued and the rule of law continued to diminish, William and Lily's parents took the decision to send their children to one of the few nations still accepting English refugees: the Shogunate of Japan. As they were both under 18, unlike their parents they could be accepted and 'naturalised'. They were devastated to be separated from their parents but filled with the relief that they could go together. They dared to hope they would be settled in the same town.

Electricity surged as his mind travelled to a more recent point in his life. They were checked, stamped, filed, indexed at checkpoints at Dover. They said numb goodbyes to their parents. The feelings had been too strong for William to allow himself to really feel. His heart hardened, his soul shrank. Only his love for Lily kept his heart and soul alive. It was too dangerous to stay. The bombings were daily now. William's mother had insisted he go, Lily's father had done the same with her. As they were still minors, the decision was legally up to the parents.

Neither of them had wanted to go, but they understood that they needed to. They held hands at the checkpoint. All they had now was each other.

They were separated at the first checkpoint in the new country. A Shogunate official in a grey uniform explained it to them in slow, enunciated English.

"You are boy," he said to William, then turned to Lily. "You are girl. Shogunate rules very clear. Boys and girls go separate. Not good to mix."

Their hands prised apart from each other. They pleaded, argued even as they were led away. The official who had spoken to them rolled his eyes and wrote on his clipboard. That was the last time they had seen each other until they had both been in the simulation when they met as if for the first time having forgotten their pasts in England.

The boys' relocation centre had been sparse and functional, a clinically clean building in the middle of a forest. They were given dire warnings of the level of obedience needed on site by the Chief Administrator. William recognised him now, he had known this man as his class Sensei, in the simulation. He remembered the high level talks he had given about the Shogunate and honour.

"The Shogunate welcomes the disciplined, strong and useful," he had said. William had played the good boy and nodded along, weighing the man up. He gave every appearance of sincerity, a true believer in the Shogunate, unlike many of the adults who were following orders out of fear.

He remembered Sensei Shirow's leniency when he had been late in the simulation. Crucially, Sensei had been unaware of the reshuffling of the reality in the simulation that had hidden the extraction of Lily. Perhaps not all officials in the Shogunate were aligned with each other. Perhaps Tagomi was acting on his own project.

In the relocation centre, Sensei had explained to William that he would briefly be put into an assimilation assessment to decide where best to place him in Shogunate society. It would be like a game and would decide if he would be an administrator, a cleaner, a soldier. All were noble occupations. All served the functioning of the Shogunate and therefore the Shogun. There had been nothing about keeping the unworthy asleep in a living death.

William realised that what the Shogunate were doing must be against international law. Would the International Community intervene if this was discovered? It would certainly cause the Shogunate to lose face with the other major powers such as Imperial Russia and United Soviet States of Europe.

Sensei had put his hand on William's shoulder, almost paternally.

"The greater good, we must always act for the greater good of the Shogunate."

But the greater good according to who?

6. The Enemy of My Enemy

William woke changed. His mind emerged from a delirium. His thoughts began to take shape – in English. A guard came into his cell and shook him, speaking in Japanese which William no longer understood. He thought in English, the only language he knew well. He would be able to speak to Lily!

"Bangashira Dono, Goro Gojima," William said insistently. "I must speak to him."

The guard grunted at him and pushed him to the floor, then left, locking the door behind him.

Later, however, Gojima's surly face appeared at the cell door. He spoke in English.

"The gaijin awakes. What do you want of me?"

"Captain Gojima, I speak to you because I want the best for the Shogunate."

"How would you know what was best?"

"I follow the vision of the Shogunate that your father and our Sensei told me of, when I met them in the simulation. This is not a vision that Matsuo Tagomi follows."

Gojima looked furious. "You dare? This is in insulting."

"Tagomi wastes resources. He kills those refugees that he decides are weak. Is it not his duty to make those who enter the Shogunate strong, rather than discarding them based on a simulation?"

"You dare much. If you were not already in line for single combat with the Machi Bugyo I would fight you myself."

"For the honour of your father who I know was a loyal subject of the Shogunate I ask you to speak to Sensei. Tell him what Tagomi is doing. Sensei is wise and is a high authority in the Shogunate, in reality more so than the school teacher he was in the simulation. You know that Tagomi has not honoured your father or you. It would be to your advantage to be on the right side."

"You presume much." Gojima slammed a fist against the cell door and departed. That went well, thought William wincing. He'd known Goro was a long shot. There was nothing for it now but to go through with the duel.

7. The Honour of Single Combat

William was taken to the Dojo in the holding complex. The Machi Bugyo, a dozen Doshin, and Lily were already there. Tagomi gave them a brief moment together to say goodbye.

"Neither of you may survive this. Say your farewells," Tagomi said.

Lily had changed, even as William regained his original language and memories. He greeted Lily and she responded in confused Japanese. Her appearance had changed too, her hair dyed black again and she wore the makeup of a geisha, even as she wore clothing suitable for combat. They embraced, both in tears. Lily's makeup ran.

"I love you," said William.

Lily responded in Japanese, but her face showed the love she still felt. Their language did not meet, but their kiss needed no explanation. It was shortlived, however as several Doshin separated them.

"She remembers you," said Tagomi. "She retains her motivation for our duel. I would not cheat Bushido by sabotaging my opponent. Her language and appearance is all that has changed. A joke I wanted to play on you, as you took your potion so you could speak the same language."

"For that insult you should fight me first."

Tagomi laughed. "She challenged me first, therefore I follow the correct order. In addition, I want you to watch her defeat."

Tagomi took up his characteristic weapon of a long staff, Lily chose to match this with a staff of her own. They bowed, then commenced the fight as the Doshin and the restrained William watched.

Lily fought bravely and passionately. She was younger

157

than Tagomi who had the edge in experience, training and brutality. He danced around her until she was exhausted, then tripped her with his staff. He brought the staff around then, hitting her on the back of the neck. Casting his staff down, he grasped her by the neck in a grim, tight hold. William cried out and renewed his struggle against his bonds but with the Doshin restraining, it was no use.

Tagomi spoke to her in Japanese:

"I have started a reaction in your body, I have used the dim mak, immobilising you and it will inevitably kill you in moments. Long enough for you to watch me kill your boyfriend."

Although William did not understand the words the situation was clear. Lily had lost, Tagomi was turning on him next.

Despite having just fought Lily, a vigorous, tiring battle for both of them, Tagomi was ready for William. The Doshin released and armed William with his chosen two katanas.

Tagomi and William bowed. William needed no words to show his fury at how Lily had been hurt. Tagomi launched into battle and attempted another sweep to trip William, but having watched Tagomi's technique in combat with Lily, he was ready and jumped. William fought with determination and passion, but momentarily lost his katana as Tagomi rapped the back of his hand hard with his staff.

With one katana left, William continued the fight, dancing around Tagomi's blows, forcing him onto the offensive, to wear him down, as Tagomi had done with Lily.

"You dishonour yourself," said Tagomi. "You forget the pain your female is in while you draw this out." The older man pursued William relentlessly around the Dojo until with a lucky strike, Tagomi disarmed him, then with another blow knocked him to the ground.

Lily screamed.

It was then that the alarms rang out and more Doshin flooded into the hall, followed by Sensei Shirow and the Bangashira Goro Gojima.

"What is the meaning of this?" asked Tagomi. "I am conducting honourable single combat. It is disrespectful to interrupt."

"You are too extreme, Tagomi san," Sensei said, helping William up. "Your interpretation of the Shogun's refugee program parametres has been illuminated and found to be inappropriate. I have spoken with the Shogun's advisers and he is embarrassed to find that you have been killing those who he had promised would be safe in his embrace."

Freed from combat with Tagomi, William scrambled to his feet and rushed over to Lily, who was fading fast. She spoke to him, small words in the Japanese he could no longer understand. He held her as she cried, eyelids fluttering like a butterfly freeing itself from a trap; she struggled against what she felt coming. He held her, himself in tears as he felt the life drain from her. "I love you," he said. But she was gone.

Tagomi and Sensei continued to argue, even as Tagomi was led away by Goro Gojima and his guards.

Sensei turned to William, putting a hand on his shoulder once more.

"I am sorry for your loss," he said. "I am sorry that I was unable to intervene before it was too late for her, but I could not act until I had consulted the Shogun's advisers. You have done the Shogunate a service by bringing this to my attention. I have been authorised to personally ensure that the refugee program will become what it always should have been, a genuine welcome to people who the country needs. The Shogunate in its generosity will treat its new subjects well. It will demand a lot in return, but it will treat them well."

8. Brave New World

Amaterasu came to William one time, before he was rehoused in the real Otaru. She was on his television. Her hair glowed; she looked like the goddess he had thought she was when they first met.

"I went beyond what Tagomi could kill," she said. "I knew that I would go to my death, so there was a back up. I live purely in the machine now. A spirit haunting the aetherial net. I have no body, but I can live in the shadows of the world, in the simulations like the one where we met. I can see through computer screens. Hear through mobile phones. I can make sure this never happens again."

"And Tagomi?" William asked. "What of him?"

"The Shogun put him on trial. Allowed him the honour of seppuku. Taking his own life by slitting his own belly."

"And me? Was Sensei truthful in his offer?"

"I'll be watching," she said. Tagomi killed my body, but I really am a goddess now. A goddess in the machine, a goddess of the dispossessed, of the refugee, and they and you will be under my protection."

William lived. At first, he could not contemplate or face life without Lily. Yet, one day at a time he rose from bed. He learned, he worked, he got through each day somehow. And so, life went on and sometimes that is the happiest ending that can be hoped for.

ABOUT M M LEWIS

M M Lewis is widely published in the independent press, including the British Fantasy Society Journal, Theaker's Quarterly and Wordland. He is currently working on a novel of urban magic. He lives by the sea in the South West of England. He is a member of the Clockhouse London Writers.

syntheticscribe.wordpress.com

THE IMMACULATE ONES

by Gary Budgen

1.

When she reached a suitable age Yasmina was given responsibilities in the orphanage where she grew up. She took the bottle of poison from beneath the sink of the wash house and spread the granules on food scraps in the places where the rats might go.

It took them a while to die and sometimes she would find one still twitching in a pool of its own vomit and bloody faeces. When it died she picked the rat up with surgical gloves and took it to the furnace in the boiler room and then go and scrub the floor where it had been.

"Why must we kill the rats?" she asked the Director.

"Because they are vermin."

"Couldn't we just drive them away?"

"Everything must die, my dear. Well, everything except the Immaculate Ones."

*

It is not easy for me to pinpoint the moment of discovery of Ultrachronia, but if feels I have been searching for as long as I can remember.

My earliest memories are of the hospital where I grew

up, the long colonnade that ran between the wing where we lived and the wards where my father worked. From the colonnade you could see down to the lake, which in memory is always still and dark, like the surface of mirror in an unlit room. It was on this lake that my sister Elodie and her lover would one day row out and shoot themselves.

My father always worked until late in the evening when I would see him treading back through the colonnade and know from the angle of his face, the pattern of lines upon it, whether another of his patients had died.

After my sister's suicide my father worked even more intensely hardly leaving the hospital wing at all, sleeping on one of the beds of the ward. I was left to my own devices, free to wander where I chose.

From The Ticket of Infinite Exchange by Charles Foix.

*

Yasmina supervised the girls' ablutions, herding them from the dormitory to the shower block, barefoot across the little courtyard hung with sheets drying on a line. They shivered in their standardised white dressing gowns each with a half-cake of soap held tightly in their hands.

In the shower block Yasmina followed the routine she had followed herself as a child, ordering the girls to leave their dressing gowns hung on the hooks outside the shower. The shower itself was one large tiled area with rows of shower heads on each side. Yasmina had to make sure each child was under one of these and that they had their soap at the ready. Then she was to turn on the faucet lever on the panel near the door. The shower would then run for a minute.

"The water's freezing," said Sally, a girl with bright red hair that sat atop her head like a tangled bird's nest.

"You must take your shower," Yasmina said. The water was always freezing on the days the Director had a long bath in the afternoon.

Sally ignored her and picked a towel up from the bench below the faucet and wrapped it around her. She began to hand round the other towels.

"Girls…" Yasmina began.

They were all wrapped but shivering.

Sally padded over to her in bare feet.

"Don't worry, Miss Yasmina," she said, "You won't get into trouble. We have had our shower haven't we?"

"I suppose you have."

*

I chose not to go out to the lake and the countryside beyond, but rather to make the house the site of my explorations. The more I explored the vaster it seemed.

I became a nomadic sleeper in that time, flopping down in the library or the long gallery with its paintings of ruffed gentlemen. In my father's rooms I embarked upon a kind of archaeology of what he had once been, finding his stamp collection, his books on chess, the walnut cabinet that contained trays of seashells, each labelled in carefully inked writing.

It was in the library that I got my first vision of Ultrachronia. Not that I had discovered any of the ancient texts upon which my work is based but rather that the library itself was a bulwark against the oblivion my father fought against. For a library is an accumulation of lost time, a preservation of things beyond decay and death.

I hardly thought of my sister but I recall a period of troubled dreams. Sleeping at the bottom of a stairwell I saw the newel post of the banister become a vast statue of myself, some idol of terrifying but unknown significance. I awoke with a sense of unimaginable loss.

I took out one of the shells out of my pocket that I had taken from the cabinet. Already I had begun to understand why I found it comforting. What is a shell if not an embodiment of the longing of even the most insignificant creature for Ultrachronia? It is the accumulation of time into nacre, of that which passes, is fleeting, into permanence.

From The Ticket of Infinite Exchange by Charles Foix.

*

Yasmina began to take some of the children's classes. She repeated the things she had been told herself when she had been like them. She showed them Government Issue slides about history and geography.

She wanted to enthuse them, make them understand that reading, even the poor material she had to hand, was a bridge to other worlds of knowledge. But perhaps she was not a very good teacher.

She looked at their faces and wondered what would happen now that the war was getting nearer and the Immaculate Ones were coming.

"Can you sing, Miss?" Tommy asked. He was a bright boy, but one who hardly ever spoke.

Had she ever sung? She thought perhaps she had, to herself…

"Please, Miss," chimed the little twins Bob and Susan.

And so she sang. A lullaby learnt from an older child long ago. Hardly remembering the words she hummed random things that she liked the sound of. And when she finished they all clapped.

*

I had loved my sister Elodie very much. It took many years to understand why she had done what she did, afloat on the lake, drinking a glass of champagne with her lover and taking up one of the pair of ornate duelling pistols.

I came to believe that they were making what might be considered an artistic statement, in line with the spirit of that time. They made their otherwise private torments public. It hardly mattered what those torments were.

Unlike the investigation into some suicides which might discover a note or a pile of unpaid bills, all my sister and her lover left behind were withered flowers from their first days together next to a pile of ashes from their love letters, all burnt but for the odd fragment containing some tender endearment.

I immersed myself in the writings of the Digital Theologians who envisaged the idea of an Omega Point where resurrection would be realised in a vast supercomputer built by humanity at the end of time.

The Digital Theologians argued that everyone who had ever lived in any possible world would be resurrected by the use of a brute force algorithm.

A brute force search checks every possible combination, which in this case means every possible combination of genome, phenotype, and personal lifeline. Given infinite time, Elodie would exist once again.

From The Ticket of Infinite Exchange by Charles Foix.

*

There were food shortages now, the official ration becoming ever stingier and missile fire sounded in the distance as the army of the Immaculate Ones drew closer. Some of the younger children had difficulty sleeping even when the missiles were not firing and Yasmina would sit in the dormitory with a lighted candle singing a lullaby.

Every morning she would take the sheets from the twins' bed and wash them, hanging them in the courtyard so that they might be dry by the evening.

One of the orderlies and two of the other nurses disappeared and Yasmina had to work harder than ever. When she sang her lullaby at night, she felt herself drifting off into a half dream until an explosion jerked her awake.

"We should leave," Sally said, twiddling with her bushy hair.

"We are safe here."

"The bombs will come soon. Then the Immaculate Ones. We need to get away."

"Now, Sally, I'm sure everything will be all right."

But Sally hung her head.

"No, Miss Yasmina, it won't be."

A few days later, the Director called the remaining staff to a meeting. Only Yasmina, the Director, and Mr and Mrs Jevit were left. The old couple managed the building and cooked.

The Director's eyes were ragged around the edges,

flecked with red. He smelt of soap and vodka.

"We all understand how difficult things have become," he said, "but if we stick together I'm sure we can do very well by the children, yes very well."

More time was spent going out to the markets by the docks to try and obtain extra rations. The Director gave her some money but it was hardly enough. Prices seemed to go up every day.

Yasmina sold some brass candlesticks, silver cutlery she found unused in the kitchen cupboard.

The sound of the missiles grew nearer, and the ground shuddered as she slept on the floor of the children's dormitory.

"We should leave," Sally said.

"Where would we go?"

*

Every age tried to understand the human mind with a metaphor drawn from its most sophisticated technology, from the hydraulic clocks of the middle ages to the telephone exchanges of the early twentieth century.

The development of information technology proved the most seductive metaphor of all, subsuming all understanding of the human mind to the point where it was impossible for some scientist to think or talk about the mind without recourse to this metaphor. Soon it ceased to be a metaphor at all.

By their circular logic, if a mind was a computer then a computer could be a mind, and a mind simulated in computer was effectively resurrection. I become disillusioned, my first attempt to understand immortality unravelling.

Yet it was just another metaphor, but one I could use

as a ladder to understanding. Much of what they described was true in the way a painting might be true of an actual landscape.

They imagined resurrection, everyone who had ever lived, who might ever have lived. I imagined that too. The ladder would always be too short. I would have to reach its top and then leap even higher. Only when I began to consider the very structure of the cosmos itself, could I see the possibility of making that leap. Not a leap of faith but neither one I could crassly call a leap of knowledge. Not yet.

From The Ticket of Infinite Exchange by Charles Foix.

*

The Director left one rain-washed morning. It was quiet, the missile fire having left off for a few hours. He stood with Yasmina on the porch out the front of the orphanage, while Mr Jevit led a small buggy that he'd managed to borrow. When he'd secured the horse, he began to load the Director's valise on the back.

"You must come with me," the Director said without conviction. "There are no trains now, not from the city. But this will get us out to the North Country."

She didn't look him in the eye, would not allow herself to be mollified by his concern for her. The night before when he told her he was leaving, she had said that they should take the children.

"There are all sorts of procedures…we would have to obtain permission…and where would we put them?"

Yasmina stood with the old man and his wife in the rain, and watched as the Director got onto the driving seat. No-one said anything and at last he shook the reigns and the buggy started off. The three of them stood there for a moment but then turned and went back into the orphanage before the buggy had even reached the end of the street.

"I'll fix you a nice cup of coffee, Miss Yasmina," said Mrs Jevit, "And bring it to your office."

"Office?"

"You're the Director now."

She thought of the children. Of Sally, Tommy, and the twins especially, whom she knew she needed as much as they needed her. Needed their faces as they listened to her, needed what they saw in her.

"I expect I am."

She sat at the desk in the office. Perhaps there was something useful here after all, contacts with the government...she hardly knew anything of that side of affairs.

The desk the photograph of the Director's wife and insipid daughter had gone from the desk. Papers were scattered around.

The top drawer of the desk had more papers, letters and memos. The bottom drawer she almost closed immediately for beneath an empty vodka bottle was a picture a woman wearing nothing more than rather fanciful underwear. There were others, a pile of them. But there was also a book.

It was bound in green cloth with gold lettering on it.

The Ticket of Infinite Exchange. Charles Foix.

Only the first two pages of the book had been cut. The Director was obviously more an appreciator of photography than books.

She closed the drawer and sat at the desk with the book as Mrs Jevit brought her coffee in.

The book must be a memento of Foix's visit to the

orphanage. Yasmin had been about fifteen.

"That is Foix," one of the other orphans had whispered, "the one who believes in an afterlife. They say if you read his book you kill yourself."

"That's silly," Yasmina had said.

Foix had been small and wizened with large round glasses that magnified the gleam of his eyes. He wore a bright purple bow tie.

Back in the kitchen Mrs Jevit was chopping meat on the table, making little cubes that would be a portion for each of the children. Yasmin found a knife and sliced open the remaining pages of the book as she watched Mrs Jevit make deft cuts.

What type of meat is it? Yasmina almost asked. But she stopped herself. These days the coffee was bitter, the bread full of sawdust and it didn't do to ask what the meat was. The rats were no longer being poisoned.

*

Even the obscenities of the so-called Immaculate Ones demonstrates a longing for Ultrachronia.

Except in their case, it has become perverted and in their endeavour to bring eternity to this world rather than strive for the next, they have made monsters of themselves.

They have made immortality a currency used by their elite to maintain their power. The promise of gaining immortality is enough to discipline an army to destroy all in its path. It is hardly a paradox that these immortals bring death to so many.

From The Ticket of Infinite Exchange by Charles Foix.

*

The bombs grew closer, moving from the outskirts of the city to nearby neighbourhoods. The vibration of the shelling shook the ground and walls, rattling crockery. The sky lit up with tracer fire and flame. The children couldn't sleep and Yasmina's voice was drowned by the noise. Yet still she tried to sing, holding the twins' hands as they whimpered.

She went to buy provisions, allotting tasks to Mr and Mrs Jevit to keep them off the streets, empty except for desperate people or those in the process of fleeing. She passed through bombed areas, rubble piles and the outlines of streets. Sometimes she no longer remembered what a particular neighbourhood had been like before, as though the missiles had obliterated not only the buildings but memory itself.

An unofficial market had appeared in the ruins of a row of terraced houses Yasmina took anything she could barter from the orphanage to get root vegetables, berries, 'meat'.

One day the market was gone and she knew it was time to leave.

They would go early, just before dawn. Luckily, that night the bombardment ended early and the children slept.

At dawn, she went out to the little yard to gather in the clothes drying on the line. She heard a blast and something like air being sliced. She was on the floor as the main building of the orphanage collapsed sending out fragments of dust and rubble and scattering the clothes on the washing line across the yard. The children wouldn't have anything clean to wear.

2.

Yasmina was found in the wreckage of the orphanage where, they told her, she had worked. Now there was no orphanage, nor any need of an orphanage, so she sang in Delilah's Garden, a nightclub, where soldiers from the Immaculate Ones' army came to gawp at her.

She lived in a hotel filled with mirrors. Rooms were cheap since much of the population had fled and there were no visitors anymore. She bought a gramophone and learnt all the songs of the records she could get.

She slept most of the day until it was time to prepare for her show. Then she put a record on and, with a glass of champagne, looked out over the city as the gaslights were lit and the ghostly glow spread through streets and the edges of rooftops.

Outside, she tried not to look at the people, who were thin, downcast, and terrified of the invading soldiers. When they saw her in her furs and jewellery, she became something hateful, flitting from gas light to gas light on her way to sing.

She saw Colonel Racine from the stage the first time, across the smoke of the nightclub. There was a crowd standing around him, the head waiter, the manager, and several officers she had been with in the past. Racine was seated, ignoring everyone who sought his attention, who were desperate to serve him in some way. Racine had eyes only at Yasmina as she sat on a high stool on the stage, her legs exposed, ready to sing.

In the dressing room, the message came as she knew it would.

There was a space around his table now, other tables moved away. He stood as she approached, and readied her seat. His uniform was impeccable, grey fabric and silver piping forming folds and shadows. Racine appeared to be in his sixties but that was just the age he became immortal. He was tall and thin, the skin on his face tight over his angular skull.

"Thank you for agreeing to join me," he said. He had their usual accent, and the slight awkwardness of speaking a language not his own. "It is such a pleasure to be with you."

She wondered that he found her presence pleasurable. How it was that someone who had done what he had done could enter a night club and look at her as he did now?

"You sang beautifully."

"Thank you."

"I have ordered champagne."

He clicked his fingers and an ice bucket with a bottle arrived instantly. The waiter poured.

"You like champagne." Not a question.

"Yes."

On stage, the comedian had started his routines. But people were only pretending to pay attention. They were watching Racine, waiting for his response.

"This comedian is not very good," said Racine, his eyes darting to the stage for a few seconds in irritation. "I think some music would be better."

"Yes, some music would be nice."

Within a minute, the comedian was gone and replaced by the house band.

"You have sung long?"

"A little while."

The band were playing an innocuous mid-tempo jazz piece.

"It is difficult for me," he said, "to be in the city when

it is like this. I came here as a young man and it ha always lurked in my memory as a place of beauty. Especially at night when the lamps are lit. Now corpses litter the rubble and the survivors are wretched, many are hungry, starving in fact."

"There have always been hungry people."

"Of course," he said, "but the starvation now is because of me. Because I have burnt your farms, confiscated supplies for my army. The streets teem with the unseemly."

"This upsets you?" she tried not to sound surprised.

"I find it indecorous."

The music stopped then started again. Racine drew out her chair.

"Come," he said, "we will dance."

She was surprised at how supple he was as he led her on the dance floor. She forced herself to relax, expressing carefully rehearsed intimations of pleasure.

No one else danced and when they were seated again, the feeling of being part of a performance was acute. Everyone was watching them, or rather watching Racine. It would be this way whenever she was with him. His presence in any room made everyone else secondary, observers ready to join in the drama that he embodied, extras to do his bidding.

That first night, he did not request that she accompany him when he left. He flicked his fingers and a waiter appeared.

"Tell them to have my car ready."

Then to Yasmina: "I must attend to some duties now. I will visit you again tomorrow."

When he rose, he bowed his head slightly and then turned to go to the door. Other officers appeared, one handing him his cape.

After he was gone, the people remaining began to talk louder, someone laughed. No one had done so while Racine had been there.

The manager sat down opposite her, picking up Racine's empty champagne flute in his stubby fingers.

"You must be very nice to him, my dear. He could be very good to us. Or very bad."

Back in her hotel room that night she studied her face in the mirror, trying to what Racine saw but she could not. She lay in bed and read, as she always did, from the book she had been found with at the wreck of the orphanage, The Ticket of Infinite Exchange.

The next morning, there was a knock on the door and the concierge bowed.

"A gift has arrived for you, madam," he said, nodding at the elaborate cage he held, and the bright green and yellow parakeet inside that was preening itself.

*

The children were on the beach. The mornings lasted as long as they desired; sunny mornings that were never too hot so as to be uncomfortable as there was always a soothing breeze bringing the tang of salt from the sea. They wandered along the sands searching among the shells of cockles and mussels, the seaweed and stranded starfish. When they found a piece of glass smoothed by the sea they would put it in a pocket.

Evening came when they wanted it to, dusk falling rapidly, the air just cool enough to warrant the lighting of a fire built with the timbers from shipwrecks that had been washed up long ago and dried in the sunshine.

It was as they sat around the campfire, in a circle of orange light, that others would come. They'd be silhouettes in the edge of darkness, nervous about coming too close. Then someone, usually Sally, would call out.

"Come closer, it's all right."

And they would, they would come closer. Always children.

They might say something.

"The soldiers came and…"

"A fire…"

"An explosion…"

It doesn't matter, someone would say, we're here now.

And they'd talk about what they had found during the day, the colour and shape of the fragments of glass. Or sometimes they'd just listen to the gentle breaking of the water on the sand, the rush of it, the foaming and retreat, and the crackle of the fire as it burnt on.

Sally thought that she had been there the longest, that perhaps there had been a time when she had been alone on the beach. The others, and there were more and more of them, looked up to her. She was the one who wandered the furthest, as though in search of something. She roamed farther and farther until one day she returned to the campfire late and told them what she had seen on the horizon, and that now was the time for them to move on.

*

That evening Racine sat where he had been before, his table given its wide berth.

After her set, she went to sit with him. The band were playing. The comedian had been fired.

"Thank you for the gift," she said.

"The bird. Do you like it?"

"Yes, I think I do."

"I thought that a monkey might take too much attention. Whereas a bird…" He waved his hand to dismiss the subject.

A solider approached, clipped his heals and handed Racine a piece of paper. Racine looked at it and then screwed it up. He put the paper in the ashtray and taking one of the books of matches set light to it. It smouldered for a bit, shot up one flare of flame and became ash.

"The book you have in your room. Foix. It is considered subversive."

"I didn't know…"

He put up his hand.

"Read it in private. And with a degree of scepticism. Many consider it the ravings of a mad man. Although not necessarily a harmless mad man. He proposes that the universe will one day ensure the immortality of everyone who has ever lived. Yet the only immortality in actuality is that which our scientists have perfected. The drug which courses though my veins. That makes me immortal. Immaculate."

"I like the parts about his life… about his sister…"

"We'll speak no more of it," Racine said, "You have to understand that it is necessary that I have eyes everywhere, that people who are close to me know I am always watching."

"Some of us are more used to being watched than others."

"Yes. You are at ease with it. That is refreshing. "

The musicians finished their number and there was faint applause. Yasmina began to clap too and it seemed others now became more enthusiastic.

"Perhaps I'll set it free," she said suddenly, "the bird."

He smiled.

"Would that offend you?" she said.

"Of course not. It belongs to you. It is your decision."

She realised she had stopped clapping and others had too.

"Come," he said rising from his chair, "I would like to take you somewhere."

There was a motorcar waiting outside, a long sedan in grey. A soldier held the door open for her. They drove towards the central part of the city so that she thought they might be going to the hotel. Here and there gas lamps were still operating, their warm glow not cutting the shadow like the lights of the car but instead fading into it, merging.

The opera house was ahead wounded by a great gash made in its dome by a missile.

"Are we going to the opera?" she asked.

"I'm afraid the voices have fallen silent. But you are being sardonic. That is good. It indicates you are feeling comfortable."

"But to the opera house then?"

"Yes, to the opera house."

*

What Sally had seen on the horizon was a building. And the moment of seeing it brought back to her the very existence of such things: of buildings and streets, walls and roofs. She could not make out the details of this building; it was far enough away to look merely like a black bar. But she knew it was a building.

The children began their journey towards it the next day.

For the first time, Sally realised, it felt as though her skin was too hot, that walking was arduous. After an hour, she let Tommy lead while she waited and checked on the other children as they passed. The twins struggled, all the way at the back. They trudged through the sand hand in hand.

"Do you want to rest?"

"We're thirsty," said Susan.

Oh that. And it all came back. The demands of the body, the need to drink and eat. That you had to have more than sunlight and sleep to survive.

"Sally," Tommy shouted up ahead. All the children had begun to gather around him, at the place where the sea foam was washing against the sand.

"Come on," she said to the twins trying to sound chirpy, "let's see what they've found."

Tommy held a shell in his hands. It was something like a large snail shell but it much bigger. The pattern on its sides looked like thin lines of orange flame.

Tommy held the shell up to his chest, and turned in a circle so that all the children could see. Some of them reached out to touch it, stroking it with their fingertips.

"Can I look?" said Bob.

Tommy smiled at Sally and then crouched a little to present the shell to Bob, who peered into the shell's opening.

"What lived in there?" he said.

"I don't know," said Tommy, "some sea creature."

"Shush," said Susan, "listen."

They all fell quiet and could hear it, a soft singing, wordless so as to be almost a hum. A lullaby coming from the shell.

*

Even in its ruin the opulence of the opera house was overwhelming. The gallery foyer was topped with panels of pinked fleshed goddesses and bordered in gold. An enormous chandelier hung dead, the gallery lit by electric lights attached to cabling stretched across the floor.

The auditorium was cold, wind coming in from the gash in the dome above, rubble scattered in places on the seats. Cabled lights lit the passage between the seating and up onto the stage. All around, tiers of private seating booths rose in circles towards the domed ceiling. Unlit, they looked like empty eye sockets.

Racine led her off to the side to an entrance onto a spiral staircase. She thought they might be going up to one of the tiers overlooking the auditorium but they kept going. Racine was remarkably fit, hardly catching his breath and only halting when they reached the very top of the staircase and entered into a circular passageway.

"This gallery runs around the dome," he said.

Windows that looked back down onto the auditorium at intervals

"Here," he said, "come."

And once more, arm in arm, he led her around the passageway until she saw the night sky up ahead where the dome had been hit by a missile during the invasion of the city, tearing a great wound in it. On one side was a fall to the auditorium and through the other they clambered over the rubble onto a flat roof.

There was a soldier waiting there by a table set with two chairs. On the table were two glasses and a strange thing: some kind of jug with a bottle in it. There was a slight wind but it wasn't cold.

"Come. Sit," said Racine.

The soldier held the chair out for her.

The object on the table appeared to be an inverted shell, like that of some huge snail with beautiful coral flames patterning it. It was mounted on heavy bronze stand carved with the reliefs of seahorses, an octopus and a narwhal.

"It is a nautilus shell," said Racine.

There was something obscene about the way the shell had been appropriated, vulgarised into an ice bucket.

The soldier lifted the champagne and poured them each a glass.

She could see across the city, and although it was dark it was lit by patches of glowing light from the gas lamps on the streets and in some of the buildings. But they were only patches for it seemed clear that much of the city was no longer occupied.

Light suddenly erupted in the distance, followed by huge shooting flames.

She stared, glass at her lips, not able to quite work out where it was...

"We are burning out the slum districts, near the industrial zone," he said.

This was what he had bought her to see.

Another burst of fire near the first.

"If you were Immaculate you would understand. We have the perspective proper to immortals. Time stretches before us and we, un-decaying, learn to appreciate the aesthetics of the decay around us. These fires are cleansing. The dirty shacks and apartments will all be razed. Then there will be a field of ash around the city with a view of the centre, of the architecture here. Soon everyone will leave and the city will begin to revert to nature. This ornate old opera house will become covered in ivy. Our work will be done, we will have produced the most beautiful of ruins."

*

Sally wanted to press on, towards the place on the horizon, where she was convinced they must go. But now that they had all begun to get hungry and thirsty, they were forced to venture inland, over the crest of the grassy dunes, to find supplies.

She had expected they would forage, find berries and a stream, but they found the entrance to a field along a short tarmacked road between overgrown hedges. A small fair had been set up. Music was playing. The smell of frying onions made their mouths water.

The children were the only customers and the stall holders in their vans were happy to give them hotdogs, burgers, candyfloss and whichever drinks they wanted, coke or cherryade. They didn't ask for money.

"We're here to help you on your way," one of them said, "or of course you could stay."

Many of the children had already run off to ride on the merry-go-round, bumper cars or the big wheel.

Sally walked around the huge park making sure she knew where each of the children was.

She watched the twins screaming with delight as they whizzed around on the waltzer.

Then she came across Tommy. He was at the edge of the fair beside a set of portable toilets that smelt of wee and poo and chemicals.

He was stood perfectly still. The giant shell rested at his feet and he was holding up something and looking into it.

"I've seen her," he said.

"What do you mean?"

"Look."

And he held the piece of sea glass up to the moonlight.

Sally could see the woman in there. She was looking

over the roof-scape of a city. There were fires everywhere, columns of black smoke rising through the glow of gas lighting.

"She's trapped in the city," Tommy said.

*

The room smelt of bird shit and smoke. There was no point in opening the window because the smell of the smoke would only get worse.

The burning had been going on for almost a week. Colonel Racine had told her to remain at the hotel, sending a staff car to take her to the club in the evenings. After they went to his own apartments, then she was returned in the morning. This part of the city was not affected by the fires directly. It would be left to become a marvellous ruin.

"What will happen to all the people?" she had asked Racine as they had looked over the city from the dome of the opera house.

"Many have already fled," he said, "others will leave. Soon we will clear the remainder. They will work on our farms or serve in the army."

"And me?"

He smiled at her. "It is in my gift to grant you what I possess. The immortality drug. You will become Immaculate and then you will come with me. To the next city, and the next."

*

The children finally reached their destination. What Sally had assumed was a single vast building turned out to be the skyline of a city. It was not a skyline she remembered, not a city with domes and spires but rather of sleek steel and glass towers in the centre, great blocks like futuristic machine parts.

As the children drew nearer to the city, the suburbs began: detached bungalows and houses on large plots of land with lawns out front.

The inhabitants came out to meet them in couples. None had children with them. They smiled with warm but detached smiles and waved their hands in greeting.

"Hello," they said. "Welcome."

"Who are you?" Sally asked a couple that approached her, a man in slacks and flowered shirt and a woman in a navy A-line skirt.

Sally was with Tommy and the twins. Other children were scattered across the lawns talking to other couples.

"We are to be your parents. We shall take you in and look after you…"

Already some of the children were being led away into the houses.

"But," said Tommy. He still held onto the shell.

"I didn't know my parents," said Sally, "but I'm sure you're not them."

"Well," said the man, "we will be excellent parents. Everything about us means we will be absolutely perfect in caring for you…"

"But we're looking…" Sally began.

The woman was leaning over Tommy.

"Why don't I take that shell," the woman said, "and we can put it safely away on a shelf in your room and you can have milk and cookies."

Tommy took a step backward, then ran.

"What is it?" the woman said.

"Come on," Sally said. She grabbed the twins and ran too, catching up with Tommy as he sped away.

185

They trotted down the broad streets lined with beautiful suburban houses, lawns covered with maple leaf fall. If they listened carefully they could hear the lullaby from the shell, could feel the weight of the sea-smoothed glass in their pockets.

A woman appeared ahead from out of the space between two houses, from beneath the shadow of a maple tree...

"It's her," said Sally, "It's Yasmina..."

But as they got nearer, Sally could see that although the woman was very like Yasmina, there was something about her that was wrong, some aspect of her face that was not quite right.

And, as though sensing this, the woman retreated back into the shadows.

"Look," said Tommy.

Another woman came out farther down the road, then another. All along the road, women were appearing. The children began to run... surely one of them must be... But each time as they neared them, they knew it was not so. They hadn't quite found her yet.

*

Yasmina returned to the orphanage in the morning. It was little more than rubble. In places, bits of wall had been propped up with scaffolding poles and brace, presumably when the bodies had been taken out. She wandered around the perimeter trying to fix herself within the building that had once been there, to remember walking through the rooms and corridors, trying to summon faces.

In the courtyard, she picked up a child's vest from washing scattered on the floor.

Then she realised why she had come here. It was not what she had thought at all.

The shower block was still intact. The cupboard beneath the sink was locked so she went out and found a piece of masonry to use as a hammer to smash the lock off.

She found the bottle of poison she had once used to murder rats inside. A ticket of infinite exchange.

I will use it on him, she told herself, put in in his drink when he isn't looking and after an hour his throat will burn, he will convulse and shit blood and vomit and die. And I will pick him up and throw him in the furnace of the boiler room.

Before she left to sing at Delilah's Garden for the last time, she lay in the bath for an hour, perhaps more. The bath grew cooler and since there was no more hot water she herself grew cooler as well as she listened to the parakeet twittering. She read from the book...

The Digital Theologians with their fondness for search algorithms might apply themselves to the problem of how each person would find another in their computerised heaven. Presumably we will locate our loved ones through some further iteration of such a brute force search...

But Ultrachronia is not a digital artefact. It is not a computer at the end of the universe. So how will people find one another? I propose the type of connection that can hardly be thought of as a search term, rather it works as memory does, through mementoes, snatches of song, the lingering moments that will somehow stay with us in the face of oblivion. This is what links one person to another. It is here that we will find our ticket of infinite exchange.

The nightclub was almost empty, the old clientele fled

or taken away. Tomorrow it would close forever when Racine led the remains of the army away.

Tonight there were a few soldiers, and staff who had been kept on for the occasion. And Racine at his table.

She wore a long white silk gown that made her look as though she were carved from ivory, and she finished her set with an old lullaby she remembered from somewhere. She had asked that a glass of champagne be bought to her so that when she had finished she could make a final toast. Racine's eyes never left her, his cold appreciation of her form unending...

She could have killed him. Somehow got the poison in his drink...

In the spotlight, she raised her glass and drank. The taste of the champagne was soothing on her ragged throat. She looked beautiful. Racine would appreciate it, would look at her as she stood there in her white dress. This was the way he wanted her forever. By his side as he crushed city after city in his immortal fervour, and amid the ruins she would be untouched, a caryatid of the rubble.

"To the memory of Delilah's Garden," she said, swaying slightly as though tipsy.

A single voice from the audience, his voice, dust blown through gravestones.

"Encore, encore."

She smiled, nodded, motioned to the musicians.

She had only sang a line when she began to gag, body reacting to the poison by trying to void her stomach. Vomit flew from her mouth and down the front of the dress as she fell to the floor.

She was glad she would not be beautiful for him. That her ruin would not be appreciated. She was glad she would never be Immaculate.

There were shouts and there seemed to be soldiers everywhere. Racine's skeletal figure loomed over her. She closed her eyes and thought of the yellow and green parakeet, wondering where it had gone after it had flown from its cage.

3.

Yasmina had sat at the table outside the café for, what felt like, all morning. She sipped her latte and when it was finished the waiter bought her another. She never grew tired of the coffee, never felt it stirring nervous irritation as she remembered it had when she drank too much. Before.

She was in the heart of a strange city and it was easier to just go along with everything than not. So much of what had happened before was not clear but the old man who had brought her here had told her that that was perfectly natural.

He had led her by the arm to the table and held the chair out for her.

"Are you to join me?" she asked when he didn't sit himself.

"I'm afraid not," he said. He smiled, light gleaming from his eyes beneath his spectacles, an old man with grey in his hair, his appearance brightened by his purple bow tie. "I have to go back to my sister, but don't worry," he said. "Your friends are coming."

"Friends?"

He bowed slightly and left.

*

The four remaining children walk on a wide motorway flyover, at last leaving the suburbs behind and entering the heart of the city with its skyscrapers.

I watch as I have watched since they arrived here. They enter the shadowed streets. Having seen the city's skyline from the suburbs, they might have expected an impersonal, antiseptic scene: clean roads and smooth tarmac, the anonymous fronts of office towers.

But it is not like that at all. Here, the heavens of myriad imaginations collide so that around the base of the skyscrapers there are older style buildings, facades of crumbling plaster in pastel shades and ornate decorated arches. Tropical shrubs in terracotta pots.

There are cafes covered with striped awnings to keep out the sun, or rather the light from above for there is no sun as such.

I left Yasmina in the café waiting and now I watch as they find her at her table. They rush to her, fold into her arms, united at last.

ABOUT GARY BUDGEN

Gary Budgen grew up and still lives in London. At various times he has been a switchboard operator, print worker, programmer, and lecturer. His fiction has been published in magazines such as Interzone and Morpheus Tales, and anthologies from Thirteen Press, Boo Books, and Eibonvale. He is a founder member of London Clockhouse Writers. His chapbook Chrysalis from Horrified Press was released in 2016.

https://garybudgen.wordpress.com/

CASTLE UNDER THE WATER

by Jule Owen

The dust was getting worse. It came in to the shop all the time now and got everywhere. Not just on the floor, where the broom and mop could reach, but on the table where Merek's uncle took the money for the things he sold. It created a gossamer film across the pages of the book where his uncle wrote down prices and the things he'd taken in barter. The dust got on the shelves too: on the tops of the old books, and the things stacked up for sale. Merek cleaned them with a dry cloth, but it was hard to get all the dirt out, no matter how hard he tried. And he did try, because he was a little frightened of his uncle.

He wasn't sure if Juhn MhHennul was related, but Merek had called him uncle all his short life. After the bombing of the town's school that left three quarters of the children dead, Merek's father had arranged for him to work at Juhn MhHennul's shop during the day. His parents both worked at the hospital; his mother was a doctor, his father a manager. His mother came home after Merek had been put to bed, and was gone before he rose. His father collected him at 6 o'clock on the dot every night or sent one of Merek's older brothers if he couldn't make it in person.

One night, no one came.

Merek sat on the step, outside the shop door which

Juhn had already closed and locked. The battered printed sign, turned to hang at "Shut", seemed as much aimed at Merek as it was aimed at customers with the temerity to come looking for bargains at such a late hour. The boy waited patiently as the other shop owners put cages across their windows and bars across their doors. The ones that did not live above their shops threw their lunch boxes and money bags in sacks over their shoulders. They headed home for the night, tipping their hats or their forelocks to Merek home.

"Your dad's late tonight," Mr Kint the owner of the bottle shop pointed out as he locked up his shop. Merek nodded mutely. It was getting chilly, and he huddled into his clothes. "Don't sit there too late, young Merek. It's cold," Mr Kint said. "You'll catch your death."

Merek watched Mr Kint disappear into the narrow alleyway. He thought about death and how he must have his very own if Mr Kint said 'your death'. And if it might be caught, then it must be constantly running away. It must be a frightened thing, like him, and that would explain why he'd never seen it. Perhaps it was hiding in the alleyway right now, shyly staring at him, ready to bolt if he approached. But then he remembered that Mr Kint said that he would catch his death if he carried on sitting where he was, so maybe his death was right by him and was invisible, or maybe it was right behind him.

He turned his head to look over his shoulder. There was nothing there but the green door with the peeling paint and the "shut" sign. Mr Kint might not have been right about the death, but he was certainly right about it being cold. It was dark too, as the sun went down and the town went into blackout. Merek put his hand in the pocket of his coat and pulled out his torch. It was the little wind-up one he had got for his last birthday, an absolute treasure to him. He wound it up carefully. The little torch threw a surprisingly bright light. He cast it around the courtyard. But then he remembered what his father had told him about using it outside at night, after curfew, and how the light might guide the bombs to his house. He quickly switched it off.

The wind rose, blowing a tin can and a discarded paper bag around the courtyard. The sound of the can echoed loudly. The window opened upstairs in Juhn MhHennul's house and the old man screeched out to the night's air, "Who the hell is making that racket?"

Another window across the courtyard opened too, and an old woman screeched back, "Keep your voice down, Juhn MhHennul! And I am surprised at you for shutting out a child in this god-forsaken place."

"What child?" Juhn said irritably.

"The doctor's child that you are paid to look after all day and make work like a slave."

"He went home hours ago."

"He is sitting on your step right now."

*

It took Juhn MhHennul several minutes to get downstairs to open the door. There were many stairs in his house, and a very winding, narrow staircase; his hips were not what they were when he was young. He waddled the last few feet through the shop, slowly slid back the bolts, and drew out the large wooden plank that he threaded through the door handles at night. Finally, he unlocked the door. As his neighbour had said, the boy was sitting on the steps.

"What are you doing here?" the old man said.

The boy turned and looked up.

Whatever sentiment Juhn MhHennul may have once had, had been crushed out of him by years of hardship, disappointment, the dust, and the constant wars and conflicts. Nevertheless, something in the uncomplaining and straightforward way the small brown-eyed boy looked up at him and said, "No one came," burrowed its way through the fortress ribcage surrounding his heart. He may also have been influenced by the judgemental gaze of his devout neighbour watching from her second-floor bedroom window, and had tea with the local priest on Wednesday afternoons. She stared openly across the narrow yard. He glanced up at her briefly as he stepped back from the door. "Well, come in then."

The old man gave the boy some of his meagre rations, and made him a cosy bed in amongst the bookcases. Merek had to climb up to this bed using a ladder, but that made it more special and compensated a tiny amount for the gnawing pain Merek felt when he thought of his father and his brothers.

As if reading his thoughts, the old man said, as he dimmed the covered lantern, "They will come tomorrow for you."

Merek nodded. If it was a lie, it was a very good lie.

The old man told the same lie the next night and the one after that, even after Juhn MhHennul knew that the hospital had been bombed and all inside killed outright, and Merek's brothers had been killed by an unexploded bomb trying to retrieve their parents' bodies from the rubble. These are not things to pass on to a child. Juhn MhHennul was not a monster. Merek began conspiring in Juhn's deception, balancing two incompatible ideas in his mind at the same time. Part of him knew his family loved him so much that the only death could keep them away, but another part clung to hope and constructed ever more elaborate stories explaining why they did not come. Sometimes, over meals, Juhn helped make these stories more concrete.

His parents were important people. They had been called away to help with another hospital in a neighbouring town. The invitation was last minute. They had taken his brothers, but had known Merek would be safe with their old family friend, Juhn MhHennul. Or the hospital where his parents worked was in a part of town that had been liberated by the rebel resistance, and his parents were now safe in a rebel camp outside of the town. This didn't explain where Merek's brothers were, but Merek was inclined to overlook inconvenient details. Or his parents had been captured by the evil ruling forces, but they were both strong and were helping other people in a prisoner of war camp. They would soon escape and come back to fetch Merek.

The shop was a box of delights in the eyes of a small child, who did not mind dust and had a thirsty curiosity. There were all kinds of objects and hardly anything new: jars, plates, boxes, cutlery, old clothes, hats, boots, shoes, glasses, ancient electronics that might or might not work, fire pokers, broken toys, flat batteries, paintings, a rolled-up moth eaten carpet, a spade, ornaments, religious votives, clocks and watches, flower pots, old newspapers and magazines, and many, many books. The shelves reached the ceiling and spanned the shop floor, so that to travel from one corner of the place to the other, a person had to navigate as if were finding their way through a maze. Juhn could walk the shop with his eyes closed, but when too many customers entered the shop at once, they often could be found in an irritated gaggle, bunched up at a dead-end, trying to disentangle themselves enough to retrace their steps.

It was a junk shop and a poor one at that, but in the middle of an unnamed war, at a time when wars were so numerous, their origins so confused that they all blurred into one, Juhn MhHennul's shop was a luxury establishment. Only the very rich could afford it, and the rich were defined as anyone who had money left over after paying for water, food, and a roof over their head.

Despite strict instructions not to play with the merchandise, at the end of every day, Merek waited until Juhn had gone up to bed. Then he would climb down the ladder and retrieve whatever treasure was marked out for night time examination. This was usually a book, which he would take beneath the blankets on his makeshift bed, and read with the help of his wind-up torch.

Juhn said some of the books in the shop were very old, and were his real treasure, because the enemies of the town – the ones that kept dropping bombs on it – did not like books. They would burn them if they found them, especially old books that said how things used to be. Now people in rich places read books on electrical devices and only kept paper books as curiosities. Except in Merek's town where no one was rich enough to afford electric books. Few were rich enough to afford the paper books in Juhn's shop either, which is why most remained on their shelves gathering dust for Merek to clean.

There were many books in the shop and they were never shelved in any order, so Merek mostly found what he wanted by accident. His mother had taught him to read. When he turned the pages of the unfamiliar, musty tomes, he imagined the pillow in his cubby hole to be her, and he was back in his own room on the other side of town, nestled in her arms, reading aloud. He did not read aloud now, for fear of waking Juhn MhHennul, but his lips moved as he read, his small fingers wandering over the pages.

One of the most fascinating books was called *A Touring Guide to Great Britain and Northern Ireland*. It was beautiful, with colour images of castles, mansions, ruined abbeys, churches, and aerial shots of imposing high cliffs lapped by azure blue seas, topped with white waves, and patchwork fields, lush forests and hills, the inland natural wonders almost supernaturally green.

He had never seen or imagined anywhere like it. His world was dust grey and beige, the colour of mud, stone walls and floors. One place in the book particularly fascinated him: a place called Arundel with a castle on a hill and the most wonderful library he had ever seen.

One night over dinner, Merek nervously asked, "Where is Great Britain and Northern Island?"

Juhn looked up from his stew and sat for a while, chewing and looking at the boy, "Have you been reading the books?"

"No," Merek said defensively, expecting to be taken to task.

But instead Juhn said, "It doesn't exist."

"But there were photographs…"

"Hah!" Juhn said. "How do you know if you haven't been reading?"

Merek looked so crushed, Juhn said more gently. "Don't read them, Merek. It's not only that you will get greasy fingerprints all over them and make them worthless, but they will make you sad."

The books were the only thing that made him happy, but saying so would only mean Juhn would stop him reading, and he didn't want to stop.

Later, after dinner was finished, Juhn helped Merek climb the ladder into his cubbyhole bed, then spent several minutes hunting for the book on Great Britain, but he couldn't find it because it was hidden under Merek's mattress of old newspapers and cushions.

When Juhn had gone, Merek retrieved the book from its hiding place, pulled the blanket over his head, switched on his torch and opened the book at one of his favourite pages titled, "Map of the British Isles".

"One day," he thought. "I will go there."

*

When Juhn MhHennul's shop was destroyed, there was no warning. It happened at night when Merek was asleep. The enemy's bombs were silent until they exploded, but when they did, the noise was deafening.

The bookshelves saved him. The roof and walls of the shop were blown to rubble and collapsed inwards, but Merek was sheltered inside his cubbyhole, and the books fell around him shielding him from shrapnel. He was buried nonetheless and was dug from the rubble, wood and books by the townspeople, as dawn broke over the town. "A miracle!" a man shouted, lifting him out. The rescue workers ran over to help.

As there was no longer any hospital in the town, he was taken to a makeshift clinic in an old factory building. He was cleaned up, his cuts and bruises seen to, a bad cut on his arm bandaged up.

"Where is Juhn?" he asked the busy volunteers that rushed past him. But no one seemed to know. Someone brought him water. "Where is Juhn MhHennul?" he asked.

"I don't know, lovey," the woman said. "No sign of him yet."

"No sign of him yet," gave Merek hope. "No sign of him yet" was like his parents who had just gone away.

Juhn had disappeared too. Perhaps he was frightened by the bomb and ran away. Perhaps he was hit on the head and lost his memory.

The people in the clinic didn't know what to do with Merek. The town was full of orphans and desperate people. No one was able to take another hungry mouth to feed. Merek could hear them discussing him in worried whispers. He didn't want to be taken home by these people. While they were still discussing him, he drank the water, put the glass carefully down on the table so as not to make any noise and slipped away.

He went back to Juhn's shop. The pub, the alleyway, the courtyard were all gone. At first, he thought he had got lost and come to the wrong place. But the old pub had been opposite the chemist which was still there, standing like a tooth in a baby's mouth, amongst rubble and destruction. Merek clambered over charred wood still warm to the touch, broken brick and concrete, roof tiles, and the contents of people's houses, everything spoilt and grey with dust. When he found where he thought Juhn's shop had been, he started to dig trying to find something he recognised. Finally, he hit upon the place where he had been pulled from the rubble. There, still wrapped in his dusty blanket was the Touring Guide of Great Britain and Ireland. He hugged it to him.

That night there was nowhere to go. He made a shelter with bits of the old bookcase and his blanket, but he was cold and hungry, and didn't sleep much. When he was very frightened, he took out his wind-up torch and looked at his book.

In the morning, one of the adults of the town spotted him, took him home, washed him and gave him something to eat. "We're a right pair," she said kindly. "I have no one left either."

"I do," Merek said. "They have just gone away."

"Yes, that's right. Just gone away."

The woman needed to go out and help with the clean-up. The raid that had destroyed Juhn's shop had flattened most of the town. "We need to try and salvage what we can," she said, as they left her house and walked down the street. "Although, honestly, I am starting to wonder why we are resisting any more. Accept there is no surrender. They do not want us alive."

"Who?" Merek asked.

"You know, the enemy."

Later, he sat quietly watching the adults dig out tins and boxed goods from the bombed-out food shop. Someone shared a cold tin of beans with him. Someone else brought him a fizzy drink. "Probably not good for you," they said. "But these days anything is better than nothing, right?"

He went home with different adults that night, a man and his wife who had lost their children. They had been teachers at his school, teaching the older children. They were kind, but he sensed their sadness, and it made him sad too.

"What's the book?" the man asked as they sat by candlelight later that night.

Merek offered it to him reluctantly.

"Where did you get this?" the man said, amazed.

"Juhn MhHennul's shop," Merek said.

"The old devil had some treasures hidden away. He should have given this to the school. He was a miserly old bastard."

"Shh! The boy. And don't speak ill of the dead," the woman said.

"Juhn's not dead!" Merek said, snatching the book back.

201

"Woah!" the man said, "That's a valuable book for a little one like you. Do you realise what it is?"

"Great Britain and Northern Ireland."

"Yes, that's right. Do you know what that means?"

"Juhn said it doesn't exist."

The man laughed. "Is that what he told you?"

Merek nodded. The man took the book and put it on a high shelf. "We should look after this," he said.

"I want my book," Merek said.

"For God's sake, Bram, don't take the boy's book."

"It's rare and probably very valuable."

"You want to sell his book?"

"I'd give him the money."

"And who is going to buy it? No one in this town. The enemy? They'd burn it." The woman got the book down. She handed it to Merek. "Here," she said, looking angrily at her husband.

*

Merek did not want to stay there anymore, where his book wasn't safe. Standing on his tip toes, he just about reached the latch on the front door. There was a blackout, as there was every night, but the moon was bright. He cast a long shadow in front of him as he walked down the deserted high street.

"We cannot hide from the moon", his mother used to say when they were huddled together in their basement waiting for the raids to start.

He had been beyond the edge of town once or twice with his parents to visit the sea a long time ago, before this war. He had only a few snatches of memories of a picnic on a blanket, making sandcastles and splashing at the edge of the water with his father. He also

202

remembered a harbour and the boats and his mother telling him that people used the boats to get to other lands.

He had been told repeatedly he must not walk in the desert. It was a dangerous place full of bad men, unexploded mines: a place where the sun beat down mercilessly, and there was no water or food. But this road also led to the world outside his village, the world where Great Britain and Northern Ireland was. That was where he wanted to go. To the green country with castles. So, after pausing at the edge of town for a few heartbeats, he stepped out into the wilderness.

It was cold so he walked fast for a long time. The road was broken tarmac and concrete with potholes filled with stones and old bricks. Every now and then, passed a burnt-out car or truck, or an abandoned building. Eventually tiredness overcame him and he approached one of these buildings. The house had only part of its roof remaining, and in the light from the moon, its windows and doors like cavernous eyes and a gaping mouth scared him. But he did not want to sleep out in the open. So instead, he found a place by the wall of the house and made a bed, as best he could, by clearing rocks from the ground. He was asleep in minutes.

A rattling, squeaking noise woke him: a thud and a bang. He scrambled to his feet. An old truck pulled up on the side of the road. It was rust coloured, with a blue patch on its right fender, the only paint that remained. A man climbed and walked towards the house. Merek raced around the back of the building. He could hear the man inside and the sound of him peeing up against a wall. Merek shoved his book inside his clothes, wedging it under his trouser belt. Then he went back in front of the house, stood by the truck and waited.

The man jumped when he saw him. "Where the hell did you spring from? You nearly gave me a heart attack!"

Merek pointed at the house.

"That place has been abandoned for years. You don't live there. Did you come from the town?"

Merek didn't respond. His heart was racing too fast and his mouth too dry. The man was totally bald with, a flat broken nose, and tattoos half way across his head, neck and on his bare arms. He wore combat clothes, like the enemy.

The man grunted. "You're very young. Where are your parents?"

But the man could not get Merek to speak. He looked about at the landscape. "You'll die out here. It's only six am and it's already thirty-eight degrees. Do you have any water?"

Merek shook his head. The man went to the truck and fetched a bottle, handing it to Merek. Merek clumsily unscrewed the top and drank from it, thirstily.

"I can't take you back to your town," the man said thoughtfully. "Your people will kill me. I can't take you to my camp either. You wouldn't do so well there. And I can't leave you here." The man sighed. "What the hell am I going to do with you?" He looked at his watch. "I need to be back at camp by noon. I'll get thrown in the locker if I'm late. I've nowhere to hide you. Do you want to stay here?"

Merek shook his head and managed to find the courage to say, "The sea."

"You want to go to the sea?"

Merek nodded.

The man considered this. "There's a town about thirty minutes' drive from here by the sea. Someone may be able to help you there." The man got into the cab, reached across and opened the door for Merek, who climbed in beside him.

"Do you know what they do to men who help the enemy?" the man asked Merek, as they drove. "They beat them, that's what. Then they stick 'em in the locker. Do you know what the locker is?" When Merek didn't respond, the man said, "Do you?"

Merek shook his head.

"It's an old building like the one where I found you, except it's got bars in the windows and doors. It stinks. They don't give you food and you sit in your own filth. All they give you is water. They keep you in there for days until you are mad. You don't want them to put me in the locker, do you?"

Merek shook his head again.

"I'll drop you on the edge of town, where no one will see me. Someone will help you. You're just a little boy. No one will care where you came from."

*

No one did.

Merek walked along the road towards the sea, and no one paid any attention to him. He made his way past shacks and makeshift shelters on the town's border, towards more permanent, sturdy buildings of brick and stone. Sand, not dust, gathered in the gutters here and the houses were not boarded up. There were glass windows and roofs with tiles rather than boards or corrugated sheets. He glimpsed the sea over the rise of the hill. It was startling blue below a cloudless sky. Had he not been parched with thirst and weak with hunger, he would have been happy to see it. He stopped outside a bakery, the smell of freshly baked bread forcing his stomach to contract. He stood for a long time watching people go in for their bread. Eventually the shop keeper came out and shooed him away. He ran around the back of the shops and hid behind the bins. After a while, it occurred to him to look inside. There were scraps. The bread wasn't fresh, but it tasted good to him. He sat until he felt less weak. He noticed a tap at the back of the building. He drank from it greedily, cupping the water with his hands. He'd never been so grateful for plain old water before.

Feeling better, he checked his book was still in his pants, and he set out more cheerfully towards the sea.

*

The streets around the harbour thronged with people and vehicles, traders, and people embarking and disembarking to and from boats of all sizes. Much bigger bodies jostled him in the crowd. No one stopped to look at him, as if he wasn't there. He found a place on the harbour wall to sit and watched the boats being unloaded.

In the late afternoon, the wind picked up and clouds rolled in off the sea. The first spots of rain sent people running from the harbour, collecting their goods, mobbing into the cafes, pubs, and doorways of shops around the harbour.

When lightning began to crack, the remaining people melted away altogether. Only the boatmen remained in the cabins of their bobbing boats, drinking from mugs and cans, and smoking pipes, patiently waiting it out.

Merek took shelter under a boat in dry dock, and leaned out upside down with his mouth open catching water dripping from the tarpaulin stretched over it.

After the storm abated, he came out and walked freely along the harbour, now free of crowds. The boatmen came out too. He sat for a moment and watched a old, grey haired man on a sailboat clear the water from the deck with a mop. He had a gnarled, sunburnt, kindly face. The man looked up.

"Want to help?" he asked. "I'll share my dinner with you?"

Merek nodded eagerly. He knew all about mopping from Juhn MhHennul's shop. He scrambled down onto the boardwalk where the boat was tied up and climbed on with the man's help. The man showed him how to push the water to an unplugged hole in the stern of the boat. There was almost an inch still in the bottom.

"I ought to get a tarp and cover up when I know the rain's coming. My back's not up to it anymore. But they're pricey!" he said. "You're a strong young thing." He leaned against the side of the boat as Merek worked, and filled and lit his pipe. "You want a job? I can't pay you much, meals, a place to sleep, maybe a few coins when I get them. I could do with the help."

Merek continued his mopping, not sure.

"Well, you think about it," the man said. After they had finished their work, the man opened the cabin doors and invited Merek below deck. It was a small boat, with a tiny galley, a table and bench, and a bed in the prow.

The man cooked tinned stew on the little stove and served it in bowls with some bread which he ripped into two chunks with his hands and put straight on the table. He got a beer for himself and a canned drink for Merek.

"It's not much, but it's something," said the man, sitting down and tucking in to his food.

"Are you from this town?" the man asked. He didn't seem to mind Merek not responding to his questions. Like most of the adults Merek had known, he just seemed happy to have someone to talk at. "I come here quite often with the boat, to bring things from the other islands and places along the coast. Occasionally, I'll do a long run across the sea. The locals don't mix with us sailors much, even though they're glad of the things we bring. They're a close lot. Surprising for people living by a port. But then, that's the wars, I guess. Makes everyone suspicious of everyone. It's hard to be that way, if you've travelled as much as I have."

*

When they had finished their meal and washed up, they went back on deck to look at the stars and for the old man to have another pipe.

"When I was young," the old man said. "I would throw bread overboard to attract the fish. I caught fish on a line for supper just over the side here." He coughed. "Can you imagine that? Me having bread to waste in such a way? There being so many fish they were just swimming about under the boat, to be pulled out on a line? So many, most people didn't bother with them. Now, you'd be lucky to pull fish up with a net in the deep ocean. There's very little out there, but sea snails and jellyfish. But you won't care about any of that. You think the way things are now, are the way they always were. And a good thing too. You had nothing to do with making it so." He looked at Merek, appraising. "Your clothes are dirty and shabby, but they were good quality once. Someone loves you. Or they did. If you want to run off home, you can, you know. I won't stop you."

Merek shook his head. "I want to stay with you," he said.

The old man continued to look at Merek carefully, and then he said, "Right you are, then." He tapped out his pipe. "Right you are."

*

The next day, the old man sat at the table in the galley looking at sea charts. Merek sat opposite him, watching patiently.

"I'm planning where to go next," the old man said. "There's someone in this town wants me to deliver some things to a place about fifty miles along the coast. Do you want to come with me?"

"Are you going to across the sea?"

The old man smiled, "Well, we'll go on the sea. But not across it."

Merek pulled his book out and put it on the table, shoving it across to the old man. "I want to go here."

The man picked up the book carefully.

"Can you take me?" Merek asked.

The man flicked through the book. "This is an old book," he said.

The boy nodded.

"There are a lot of different places in here. Is there somewhere in particular you want to go to?"

Merek's face lit up. He hurried over to where the man was sitting and turned the pages until he found Arundel. "There," he said. "Someone told me it doesn't exist."

"Oh, it exists alright," the old man said.

"Is the castle still there?"

The old man hesitated and then said, "Yes."

"Have you been there?"

"I've passed by."

"Is it a long way away?"

"It's a fair journey from here, but nothing we can't manage," the man said. "It's important to you, to see this?" the old man said.

Merek nodded.

The man said. "Then we'll go. After we've made our delivery, though. We have to earn money to eat before we can have adventures."

Merek liked working on the boat. He liked the little outboard motor that put-putted as it pushed them out from the harbour to where they could pick up a wind. He liked the sails that the old man hoisted expertly, and the sound of them flapping in the wind. He liked the sound the water made on the bottom of the boat when they weighed anchor later that day, further up the coast, just off shore. There were no lights from the land. The people, the old man said, had long since left the villages and towns along this part of the coast. Away from street light and the light from houses, the stars were very bright.

*

They reached the destination for their delivery the day after that. There was no port. The old man dropped his dingy into the water and got down into it, with his oars. He asked Merek to pass down the boxes of things to be delivered. "I'm to meet the man on the shore over there," he said. "No point in you coming. No point in anyone knowing about you."

An hour later he was back in the boat and hoisting the sails.

They sailed for two days, hugging the coast, making stops at night in sheltered bays, and eating from tins heated up in the galley.

"How far do we have to go?" Merek asked the next morning, as they set off.

"We'll be there in an hour."

"But we haven't sailed across the sea."

The old man smiled. "The sea is all around you."

"Are we really going to Arundel?" the boy asked.

"Yes."

*

They were far from the coast when the old man lowered the sails. It was a fine day and although there was a wind, it was gentle and warm.

"Why are we stopping here?" the boy asked. "Should I lower the anchor?"

"No, no. We want to float, so we can see it."

"See what?"

The old man was looking over the side of the boat. He beckoned Merek over. "Come look."

Merek looked down. The sea was very clear and it was possible to see below for a long way.

The very top of the castle was not so far down. The turret of one of the round towers was distinct, its grey stone pristine in the dead water.

They spent forty minutes floating back and forth over the castle, sometimes using the little engine to correct course. They looked at the old medieval town, too, and the gothic cathedral.

"We need to go back to shore now, lad," the old man said finally. "I can see clouds over there. They don't look like friendly ones."

They found a bay and anchored close to shore, safe inside the cabin when the rain came down.

"Is it all under water, then?" Merek asked later, when they were eating their stew. "Great Britain and Northern Ireland?"

"Not all of it. This coast is what people used to call Britain and all the land and the desert beyond it. It just looks different now and has a different name. The sea has taken much of the land and the sun has burned away the grass and the trees."

"When?"

"A long time ago."

"So my book is wrong?"

"Not wrong. Just very old. Are you sad?"

Merek nodded.

"Me too," the old man said. He got up from the table and cleared away the dishes.

"Is there anywhere left that's like it?" Merek asked.

"Now there's a question," the old man said. "Maybe in the far north. I don't know. I never go that far."

"I will go," Merek said. "One day."

ABOUT JULE OWEN

Jule Owen was born in the north of England in a little place nestled between Snowdonia, the Irish Sea and the Pennines. She now lives in London where the weather is warmer and there are more museums. By day she is a practising digital technologist, working on products that involve machine learning and automation. By night and weekend, Jule is a science fiction author with a passion for science and a terror of climate change. She's the author of three published science fiction novels and the writer of short stories about the near future.

www.juleowen.com
Twitter: @juleowen
https://www.facebook.com/juleowenwriter/

REGOLITH

by MJ Rodda

Sun and dust. Sun and dust was all there ever was, and all there would ever be.

He stood exposed beneath the sun that dominated everything, pinning him down like a collector's moth in a display box. Even at full attenuation, glare leaked through the filters on his old visor where the dust had ground away at the exterior surface. He could never escape from the dust, the smoky regolith, pulverised by billions of years of impacts and electrically charged by the solar bombardment so that it stuck to everything and got into everywhere, no matter how hard he washed or how assiduous his anti-static regime. The dust was a permanent second skin.

At night, when he scraped the blunt back of a knife across his skin, a grey-black gunge – a composite of lunar regolith and his own sweat – accumulated on its edge. His nights had once been agony, laid spread-eagled to give relief to the stinging skin in his armpits and groin rubbed raw by the dust. But that skin had long since thickened through repeated abrasion. All he felt now was the gritty rubbing against the inside of the suit. Dust was hard to manage at the best of times. The privileged population struggled in their shiny new suits; his was an antique.

He made his way to the digger. The trench he was digging, and subsequently filling in, was now almost half a kilometre from the airlock of his little dome. It had been a luxury dome in its day – a wealthy family's folly – set up on a private patch of the surface, independent from the cities, for picnics under the stars.

His home: over five hundred kilometres from the nearest human settlement, older than his suit, with ancient, cracked solar panels caked in regolith. The court had jerry-rigged new panels that mostly worked, and stopped him from boiling alive or freezing to death. They extended from the outer surface of the dome like broken insect wings. When the drones flew in with their cases of military rations and sanitation supplies, they looked like wasps circling a dead beetle.

They had said to him that he could stay there until he died, or he could dig his trench, and maybe they'd set him free, assuming he didn't die first anyway. An early death looked likely, since both his dome and the digger's control room leaked increasing amounts of air, and provided scant protection from solar radiation.

Still, the chance to be free, to see people again, after five years of incarceration and now two long years, alone and digging…

Earth hung low over the eastern horizon, gleaming blue like an improbable gem. Maybe one day he'd go back, and eat Italian food and drink German beer.

The dome sat in a crater which had a flat bottom with sides that rose steeply at the edge. The path out followed a curving line, traversing up the north side of the crater, minimising the gradient, but still a tough climb in a heavy, unassisted suit. The crater was the largest for a hundred kilometres in any direction, a part of the eastern edge of the Sea of Fecundity, so that when he finally clambered to the top of the crater edge, the view of this relatively flat corner of the arid sea was commanding. His digger sat by the trench like a Victorian dockyard crane. The digging arm, a boxy, articulated trellis with a gaping mouth pointed towards the sky. The cab was like the boiler of a steam train, held together with great bolts and covered with an antique, weathered patina.

The operator had a good view of his work from the front quadrant, three metres above the surface. Other machines could have dug the trench in a fraction of the time, but that would not be a prison sentence.

The trench started with a downward slope, into the excavated regolith. The digger had limited downward reach, so the incline was necessary to drive into the trench.

Every day, he drove the trench forward, scraping at the advancing rock face, five metres deep and six metres wide, lifting the removed material to form two ridges of dust and rock along the edge, which would be pushed back into the trench upon completion.

Fifty metres away, in the contorted foothills a vast mountain of bodies began: almost one hundred thousand human beings, frozen hard in the lunar vacuum.

For the purposes of simple calculation, it can be assumed that a human body is two metres long. This is above average height, but a convenient estimate when digging, thus giving a certain amount of leeway to the project. If he laid each body lengthways across the trench, he could fit three bodies, head-to-toe, across the six metre width. Layering the bodies vertically would be unwise at such a shallow depth, and the limited reach of the digger's arm meant that he could not excavate beyond five metres, without having to leave the trench entirely to deposit removed material.

He gave each body a half-metre's width. A grid of nine bodies was six metres long and a metre and a half wide. There were ninety-nine thousand, three hundred and eighty-six bodies to be buried. Side by side, in a single line, they would form a line nearly fifty kilometres long. Burying them head to toe in threes would mean a trench a third of that distance. And so his sentence was determined: dig a trench five metres deep, six metres wide and nearly seventeen kilometres long, removing almost fifty thousand cubic metres of material in the process.

He took a sip of bitter water from the straw that protruded into his helmet. The grit ground between his teeth. Nasty stuff, this moon dust. Carcinogenic, and since it carried an electric charge, it stuck to everything.

Sand and dust on Earth was formed through marine erosion, each grain was smooth and round. Lunar soil was formed by impacts that smashed rock to pieces. Each grain, even the tiny, cigarette smoke-sized particles, was sharp and jagged.

Once it got into your system, it tore away at your cells. There was only so much damage of a human could take before his cells started going wrong. The leaking, failing equipment let in more and more of this dust every day; he was saturated with it, inside and out. How long would he have left once he was free, before an evil tumour appeared? Maybe it was a part of the sentence to make him live here, exposed, then let him die in agony in ten years. He wouldn't give them that. No long, slow death for him. He wouldn't stay in the dome to die, he'd dig his way to freedom and if his future held a gruesome death, he'd cheat that, too.

Just do this one thing, and he might win his freedom in less than a year and a half. All he had to do was bury nearly one hundred thousand human beings.

*

Freedom was a relative concept. He doubted he would ever be truly free. The potential brevity of his sentence felt like a publicity stunt, something to keep the baying crowd satisfied: an ironic punishment. There was no chance he would have a choice in where he lived, or who he met with.

His every movement would be monitored, but at least he would be on Earth, away from the dust. Maybe they would let him have an apartment, and bring the odd girl back. He might have to assume a new identity.

There would be many people who disagreed with his sentence, and would want him to spend his whole life in jail, or maybe thrown out of an airlock. A new name, maybe a new face.

Maybe he could be like normal people, reading the morning news screen, going to local bars, talking football and flowers with the neighbour.

In a sense, he'd done the State a great service. Once they captured him, after the Pegasus Dome had been destroyed, they'd squeezed everything out of him that he knew about Lunar Liberty. It wasn't a question of resistance; he hadn't broken under torture, although he had felt pretty unpleasant for a few days. They'd drilled in to his memory with chemicals and magnetic scanners, and physically extracted his knowledge, in chunks.

He was convinced that bits of his brain had been killed or removed. He had trouble recalling names and faces of his previous life. They'd shown him news footage of people arrested thanks to his testimony, but he hadn't recognised any of them.

There had been some executions, via the old airlock method. It became something iconic in the movement.

Some protestors wore necklaces or brooches with tiny figurines of people curled up in the foetal position: the instinctive position someone takes when thrown into the vacuum, as if the body is trying to stop the gases it contains from bursting into space.

But execute too many people by airlock and don't give enough thought to orbital mechanics, and they could end up in permanent orbit, either of Earth, Moon or Sun, which was unsightly at best and potentially dangerous.

Standard practice was to strap a little explosive body pack to the naked, restrained victim, throw them in to space, fire up the pack, and boost them up to few dozen kilometres per second, heading out of the plane of the ecliptic.

Millions of years hence, any aliens who would happen across them would be able to follow them back to Earth like a trail of candy.

He'd escaped such a fate, mostly due to the haul of intelligence from his mind, but also because of his popular punishment.

*

The Lunar sky troubled him; it was too big, too much to take in.

Before, he'd been able to escape, either by spending his time in the domed cities or heavily filtering his visor. Out here, though, with ancient, creaky equipment, it was difficult to escape. His mind tried to latch onto the stars as objects, but was swamped by the distance, by the numbers. The Milky Way hung above like a serpent, as big as a god. He was getting used to it. He was learning how to not react to the vastness of it, by making himself transparent to its enormity. He supposed he'd always been inward looking, concerned with his life and the lives of those he cared about. The caprice of reality sits ill with the revolutionary, especially writ cosmically across the sky.

Once he'd trained himself to endure the sky, he'd had to train himself to endure the monotony. Day after day, cutting through the grey earth in patterns repeated thousands upon thousands of times.

He remembered moving to the Moon when he was a teenager. His father had mined the deuterium that was such an abundant ingredient of the regolith. His father had been a miner on Earth, originally, and a very successful one at that. He'd been raised in a fine old house in Highgate, on a hill overlooking London.

His father was almost never there – always on some tour of the Solar System, or going to the Asteroid Belt searching for minerals long since been depleted on Earth.

His mother was a glamorous figure, something of a London socialite. He remembered the parties, being in bed while music, laughter, and aromatic smoke percolated up to his room. She worked – something to do with fashion.

One day his father came home, and greeted him at the door with an awkward hug. He was fourteen at the time, already the taller of the two, and they hadn't seen each other for over two years. His mother had kissed his father, also awkwardly. That night, he'd heard them arguing while he lay in bed. It was a serious one from the tone, but he could make out nothing of the words, muffled through two stories of the house.

The next day there had been a family meeting. They sat around the kitchen table, his mother looking grim, legs crossed, staring at a cup of coffee while she stirred it with a teaspoon. He remembered her elaborate nail polish, each nail stencilled with a tiny, white Chinese dragon on a red background. His father wore a suit. He'd be working, spending twelve hours or more a day at the company's London offices.

He had big news. Important news. Exciting news.

They were moving to the Moon. He was to take charge of the deuterium mining operation his company were setting up in New Berlin, in the Northern Highlands. New Berlin was the biggest of the twelve domed cities; two hundred thousand residents, the capital of the Moon. The material wealth of the regolith was only just beginning to be exploited, he had said, and this was an opportunity they couldn't afford to miss. If he played his cards right, his father had told him, he could work for the company too, and be set up for life.

So they'd moved to the Moon. From the time they'd arrived, he had loved it. New Berlin was the most exciting place he'd ever been. The company was investing plenty of money in the operation, so a lot of people were moving; young families, mostly. The company sponsored university students, a scheme his father had participated in, and many of the graduates of his father's generation were moving to the Moon, and bringing their families with them. He'd always been an

easy-going character, able to get along with anyone. He remembered his grandmother saying to him once with pride that he had been blessed with the ability to see the good in everyone. He was popular, known by most of the kids at his school.

They would spend their Saturdays gliding in the parks – you could buy a wing suit that was entirely muscle-powered, and get yourself into the air with your own efforts in the combination of low gravity and high air pressure under the dome. Crystal Park, the largest in New

Berlin, had a fifty-foot-tall escarpment running down one side, a natural feature of the landscape that the builders had incorporated into the design of the park, greening it with imported foliage. Buddleia, especially, seemed to thrive in the low gravity, so that the foliated side of the escarpment was streaked with purple and blue.

He and his friends would climb to the top, and throw themselves off in their wingsuits, gliding effortlessly, using trees as the marker points for racing.

They played moonball, mostly for the comedy of it. Nobody could keep their balance if an attempt was made to kick the ball with any force. Most moonball games ended in laughter as players lost control of their momentum, and ended up somersaulting backwards.

Their home was modest by London standards – by necessity. Space was at a premium in the domed cities. New Berlin wasn't as large as it was possible to make a dome, not by a long way. Theoretically, with nanotube construction, you could roof the entire surface of the Moon in an unbroken sheet. But for every square metre of ground that a dome's footprint increased, the construction cost spiralled exponentially.

Few people had gardens – only the very wealthy – and his father wasn't that, at least not yet. Still, they had a decently sized two bedroom apartment with a fine view of one of the smaller parks out of the living room window.

His father was as busy as he ever had been, spending all his time at the office or whichever rock face it had happened to be important that week. His mother hated it. Clothing and fashion on the Moon was utilitarian; she stood out in her impractical, brightly coloured clothes. Even a top quality dome like New Berlin was not immune to the ingress of Lunar dust, which, by its nature, tended to rend at clothing at a microscopic level, wearing things out more quickly than on Earth.

Pretty soon, her expensive wardrobe was ruined, and she bitterly assented to wearing more practical, but duller, clothing. Within his mother's earshot, his father said fashion was decadent and unnecessary, and it didn't really matter what people wore. His mother had disagreed, vehemently, describing fashion as an expression of one's personality. His father said, "There's no space for personality on the Moon".

His mother was bored and lonely. She had gone from London, one of the great cities of the World, to a backwater. Living in a city of a couple of hundred thousand rather than millions was a culture shock for her.

"Just join the local social club," his father said. He sometimes thought that his father didn't understand his mother at all.

One day, he got home from school to find a note on the kitchen table. His father was at work (where else?), and there were instructions for dinner, which his mother had left in the fridge. The note ended: I've moved back to London. Come and visit. I love you, Mum x. From the look on his father's face, later that night when he finally got home from work, the letter he had received wasn't quite so affectionate.

*

Even then, it had not been utopia on the Moon. New Berlin was wealthy, and so were some of the lesser domes, but others were not doing as well.

Even within New Berlin, there was disquiet, and the spectre of poverty. The oldest domes, settled over a century ago, were almost destitute, requiring government grants just to keep the lights on and the dome sealed against the vacuum. They'd been built at the poles, taking advantage of the regions of eternal darkness where the sun was forever blocked by the topography.

As the building extended beyond the poles, the original settlements became more and more marginalised, economically. And yet they persisted, instead of being abandoned.

Second and third generation settlers lived there, whose identity was tied to that early polar existence. The Polars had a lot of sympathy from some of the older equatorial cities. Lunar Patriotism was emerging.

In the years after his mother left, he stayed on the Moon visiting her mother occasionally, usually every other Christmas. She soon found a new partner, and the divorce was swift. Neither were particularly interested in events on the Moon, and whenever he was on Earth, he soon pined for the spaces of New Berlin again, not to mention the low gravity. Spending any time on Earth was exhausting; he felt defeated by its massive pull.

On the Moon he was free. His father paid him minimal attention, since he was always working. He'd grown independent of his father, only enduring the odd lecture about his failing grades. He was becoming less and less interested in school, or the possibility of working for the mining company. He travelled a lot.

He visited all the domes, and went to the isolated polar cities. It wasn't that easy to get to them, flights were few and far between, and expensive.

He got some connecting flights, and hired an old rover to take him the last couple of hundred kilometres. He had gone with a friend; it had been like a camping trip.

They'd arrived at the old North Pole dome, sunk within its crater, as if it had been there for centuries, the outer layer was caked in grimy regolith. The panes towards the base had been partially cleared of dust by a cursory clean. Internal light shone out through cracks and holes in the dirt and dust, giving it the appearance of muslin draped over a lightbulb.

Inside, the ancient town was covered in dust. It hung in the air like smog. The buildings, once the white of the old NASA Lunar settlements, were shaped like cones with the tips cut off. Everyone wore environment suits – it was no longer safe to walk around in the dome unprotected and breathe the air. They'd been hooked up with a local family by a gap-year travel company. The mother – a robust looking woman in her late fifties – explained how they existed in the wasteland: the Polars had dug themselves in.

She led them into the capsule-like dwelling, but this turned out to be only a surface cap of a large underground structure – a bunker, almost. The tunnels and shafts, hacked out of the rock over the decades, now stretched beyond the footprint of the dome itself, a means by which the population had managed to increase their living space without having to increase the dome size.

The ridge of the crater in which the dome sat was lined with thousands upon thousands of square metres of solar panels – they never lacked for energy. But, even though they could survive, and keep the regolith at bay in their underground chambers, and redirect the sun to grow their crops, they were forgotten and lived in poverty.

He had travelled to the various equatorial domes. There were few settlements at the latitudes that on Earth would have been called 'temperate'; once the technology existed to resist the day and night time temperatures, there was no point not building at the equator, since this was where most of the solar energy fell.

The result was a ring of settlements around the waist of the Moon. Many had once been mining settlements, but had since become residential towns, struggling with their own economic problems as the local mining had been exhausted, and the people left behind.

There was a general sense that the big mining companies came in to an area, founded a settlement, encouraged employees to work for them there with generous wages, then abandoned them to their fate when they moved on to new areas.

This wasn't true for the best engineers, no doubt, but most people had come for a better life. The drivers of the machines, the diggers, the workers in the processing plants – if a new settlement job was not available to them, were told to go back to Earth.

But by then, roots had been set down, children born and raised, family history created. Many of them loved the Moon. It was their home. Amazing how swiftly a sense of nationhood is created, a sense of propriety. The wealth of the Moon should be for all, they said. It was being plundered by a faceless corporation, they said, and the profits taken back to Earth.

He had felt these arguments, they pulled at him, even though he'd only been on the Moon a short while. The crony capitalism of Earth existed only to enrich a tiny minority, when material wealth was abundant all around them.

So, he started attending political meetings. At first, they had been desperate and disorganised, often with multiple groups having different aims. One group, the far-right, ridiculously named Lunar Warriors, advocated extreme immigration control, with only those born on the Moon and their families given the rights to living space.

The practical difficulty of eviction in a vacuum and its grizzly consequences put paid to that idea, and besides, most people didn't feel that strength of hate. They just wanted a fair deal.

The meetings he'd mostly gone to were organised like old labour unions, with simple demands made of the mining corporations. The main issue was compensation for a terminated contract. If the mining dried up in an area, and the workers couldn't be moved somewhere new, they wanted fair compensations for all the upheaval they'd gone through to move there in the first place.

It wasn't greed, they said, it was just the means to start again, and not be left destitute. The companies told them to move back to Earth and look for work there, but in many cases, they did not have the money to pay for the flight. Even with all their technology, flights to and from the Moon were not trivial affairs.

The intransigence of the companies was a shock to everyone. With no general Lunar government to fight their case, the people of the Moon were dealing with money-making entities unfettered by law or legal precedent.

In the absence of laws prohibiting unethical behaviour, the path to greatest profit was the path always chosen. Some people from inside the corporations even had sympathy for the Lunar population. But the companies, driven from boards of directors in London or New York, simply viewed the Lunar unrest as a problem to be navigated, not unlike unstable geology. And the hungry factories of Earth didn't know or care about the provenance of the materials they consumed.

One day, his father confronted him about his attendance at one of these meetings. He was nineteen years old, and a conflict had been brewing between them

227

about his future. Somehow, his father had discovered what he had been doing with his spare time – and he had a lot of spare time, being unemployed and dependent on the charity of others.

People were charitable, too, especially as he was starting to do so much work for the Unions. He was a good organiser, and while the Unions were not yet organised or professional enough to employ him, still, he worked hard for them, arranging meetings, going door to door with leaflets, helping out in the soup kitchens for those who had lost their homes and had to sleep under the glare of the hard Lunar sky, shining through the dome.

His father, insulated, of course, from the problems experienced by the general population by a big pension and guaranteed work on Earth when the mining dried up, told him he was wasting his life. He told him the Unions were a fiction, a made-up political entity with no power and no bargaining position. Just a bunch of people sitting around complaining, when they should be heading back to Earth to look for work.

So, the next day, he'd left. He waited for his father to leave for work in the morning, had packed his bags, and walked out. Immediately, he felt foolish. In such a small population, he was sure that his father would be able to find him. But you never knew, he was pretty sure he'd find plenty of people who would give him shelter. Besides, there were no police on the Moon, only the security details for company employees. That was another contentious issue.

Once a company left, they stopped paying for security, and populations found themselves in a lawless community, forced to form scratch militias and kangaroo courts. Crime usually spiked, due to the general increase in poverty.

He moved from dome to dome, city to city, over the next few years, building contacts and helping to make his activist community more cohesive. He didn't really live anywhere. He thought of Earth less and less, even though it hung in the sky, a luminous blue ball.

If he did have a home on the domes, it was in Caledonia, one of the oldest equatorial settlements, about a third of the size of New Berlin. Caledonia had been hit hard by the closure of the local mine, and the resulting official abandonment of the dome, but they were doing better than most.

The dome had been designed to be agriculturally self-sufficient, and its giant hydroponic growing towers fed the modest population. It became a hub, of sorts, for the various political movements to meet, since it was far from New Berlin (about a quarter of the way round the Moon), and still in relatively good order. But still, most of the population were unemployed.

It was here that he helped, in his small way, to start to bring these disparate, discontented groups together into a cohesive whole. They called themselves Lunar Liberty. Some had said it should be Opportunity, since it wasn't as if they were being actively oppressed; they had just been ignored. Lunar Liberty had been chosen for, amongst other things, the effect if would have on the population of Earth, the people there being familiar with stories of national liberation. They began to draw up their demands.

But they were dealing with forces they could not imagine. The Moon was seen as a part of the territory of Earth, and so was as broken up, legally, as the nations of Earth were.

Treaties had been drawn up, centuries before, allocating the regions of the Moon to different countries of Earth. Such and such crater was American, some part of a sea was Chinese, or Indian, etc.

The people of the Moon were barely aware of these distinctions, having a shared Lunar identity, but to the Earth nations involved, it appeared as though a migrant, poverty stricken population was attempting to set up home on a piece of their sovereign territory.

The demands of the Lunar people were being relayed not to a single government, but to a dozen different countries, all of whom had a vested interest in the continued and uninterrupted supply of Lunar minerals.

They had no representative on Earth, no seat at the high table. All of their simple demands, without exception, were ignored, with threats of security intervention if any mining infrastructure was interfered with. This implied accusation was a shock to many of them. *So, they think we're terrorists, do they?*

The rift between the Lunar population and the nations of Earth, already wide, became wider still, mostly due to a misunderstanding of motive.

Few people travelled from Earth to see the situation for themselves, and the few journalists who did, found themselves labelled as 'liberals' and 'do-gooders'.

The population saw the tabloid headlines from places like the UK and USA. 'Mooners', they were called, portrayed as a sort of parasite population, interfering with the good intentions of the mining companies.

There was a general split developing within Lunar Liberty. From somewhere, at the back of the room, as it were, or out of the corner of their eyes, thoughts of violent action could be felt.

The more sober realised their hopelessly vulnerable position, but emotions, being what they are, overrode this rational assessment and yearned for action. His mind had been set on following the action.

Out of Lunar Liberty was born the Lunar Liberation Front, and he gladly signed up. Looking back on it, he is amazed at how ignorant and naive they all were about their profound vulnerability.

Those who preached peace were ignored. They formed a plan that they thought would send a message to the governments of Earth. A message that said what? That they meant business? The LLF began to arm itself. Guns were impossible to come by in quantity and a foolish item to own in an environment inches away from oblivion.

Not even the security details of the mining ships carried them. Those had electric prods, and other non-lethal weapons. Explosives, though, they could be made.

He remembered one particularly fractious meeting, where the split between the LLF and Liberty was deepened, beyond repair, as many realised at the time. Liberty members regarded explosives with utter horror, seeing in them their entire destruction. But it was so wasteful, too.

The surface of the Moon was nitrogen depleted. All nitrogen had to be carefully fixed from supplies brought in from asteroids. Without the resources to capture their own asteroids, they were dependent on what the mining ships brought with them. Nitrogen was precious – without it, and the careful management of its cycle, Lunar agriculture would fail. To see the priceless nitrogen literally blown apart was, in the minds of the Liberty faction, criminally irresponsible. In return, the LLF accused Liberty of lacking the nerve for the inevitable fight that was coming.

So he helped to make bombs, taking nitrogen and other nutrients from the very soil. They had yet to decide what they were going to do with the bombs, but it felt powerful to have a stash of them.

There were various candidate targets, the general consensus being that any attack should be against assets far from the domes, lest a catastrophic accident occur.

In the end, a target was found: a great launch ferry with enormous engines that had the power to lift large loads into orbit for transfer to a waiting transit ship for delivery to Earth.

The ferry would then return to the Moon and the cycle would continue. It was a good target. If they could hit it when it was rendezvousing with the transit ship, they could destroy both, and since both vehicles had few crew, the loss of life would be minimal.

He volunteered for the mission, and during the long Lunar night, he ventured out with four others, old night vision equipment attached to their visors. They drove towards the launch site, the giant rocket looming in front of them, glowing green through the image enhancement.

It launched during the Lunar day: it was dangerous to launch during the Lunar night. The site appeared deserted: no perimeter fence and few staff.

Lights shone through the windows of the hermetically sealed buildings, so they approached the rocket from the opposite side.

It never occurred to the transit company that anyone would try to destroy a shipment, or even steal one. What use would there be for unprocessed deuterium or helium-3 or selenium or bismuth or whatever, if there was no way to get it off-Moon?

The loading and launch pad was devoid of humans, the rocket's bays loaded by the dumbest of robots. A stream of robotic lifters carried pallets from a warehouse, along a paved road to the launch pad where a crane lifted them to the level of the rocket's clam-shell bay doors.

Another robot lifted the pallets, and then disappeared inside the hull. The rocket was as tall as an Earth skyscraper but much broader. Huge, tubular engines clustered around the edge of its circular base.

The pallets on the warehouse floor were split into canisters with simple aluminium plates for lids, held in place with latches.

He stood near the door, waiting and watching in case their intelligence had been wrong, but there was no one there. No one but the robots and they weren't paying attention.

He slipped in, followed by the others, and then it was a simple matter to walk alongside these pallets, prised off the lids, take out the contents, and fill up the space with explosives.

In this way, they filled the top layers of six pallets with explosives. They loaded the rover with the material they were to discard, which they dumped later into the skylight of a local lava tube. Each set of explosives had a remote detonator, tuned to the same signal capable of being triggered from the ground by radio. The robots dutifully and ignorantly loaded their pallets.

They'd planned to observe the rocket through a stolen telescope and detonate the explosives when it rendezvoused with the transit vehicle. But they lost sight of the tiny dot against the black sky when it was less than a third of the way to its destination. So, they went on timings instead.

It was a tense time, sat in the shadow of a crater wall in a rover. Their telescope focused on the spot where they thought the rendezvous would take place. The feed on the rover screen showed only black night.

Three hours and six minutes into their wait, light flickered on the screen. He reviewed the footage repeatedly, but it was difficult to determine the cause. Sunlight reflecting on some orbiting detritus? A glitch in the telescope, or in the computer's image processor? At a distance of many hundreds of miles, it was a handful of pixels of the image, too few and few for the human eye to resolve.

Shortly after, the frenzy of radio traffic left them in no doubt – the two ships had been destroyed.

*

The swift response startled him. He'd assumed that the Lunar system was as unguarded as anything on the surface. He hadn't expected to see a reaction within the day. He learned later that an Earth ship on its way to Europa was in close proximity to the Moon.

He was making for the Pegasus dome, working his way with the others over the cracked terrain of a meteor shower basin. Pegasus loomed closer, dipping up and down in the viewscreen as they slewed in and out of small, shallow craters.

A burst of bright light flashed directly ahead, so bright that it overloaded the rover's imaging systems, which went white, then black, as they failed to cope with the incoming radiation. Minutes later, the rover flipped upside down as a shock wave passed through the Lunar soil like a wave in a pond. Two of the team were killed. When he managed to crawl out of the stricken rover, he found the Pegasus dome had been cracked open like a boiled egg with its top cut off.

He finished the trench in the late Lunar evening. The slanting light from the sun failed to illuminate the bottom of it, so the eye could fancy that it had no floor, and was a gash made by a giant's knife in the soil of the Moon.

He felt flat. Should he feel pride in its completion, or dread at his next task? He suspected his emotions were unreliable, since his brain had been tampered with, and his subsequent isolation with nothing but hideous mound of bodies for company.

In the small garage on the side of his little dome, where he kept his tools and other useful items, was the tool by which he would move on to his next task. Instead of a bucket, his digger was now equipped with a hydraulic claw, with which he would pick up human bodies in clumps and drop them in to the trench. He started at the end of the trench furthest from the mountain of bodies.

Drive to the mountain. Drive in the claw. Close the claw. Withdraw with three or four contorted, grotesque human figures. Drive to the end of the trench. Drive back. Collect more bodies.

A fleet of drones could accomplish the task in hours, and there was no real need to dig a trench at all. There were lava flow skylights, or deep craters, or even isolated patches on the far side of the Moon where it was unlikely anyone would ever see them again.

But this was his allotted punishment, and if he didn't carry out these instructions, they'd simply cut off his food supply, or kill him outright.

Besides, this was the path to freedom, and it wasn't so bad. Maybe, biologically speaking, it was the best thing one could do with so many corpses.

For billions of years, the Lunar regolith had been

bombarded with solar wind, ionising and charging it, but also sputtering it. Bits of matter knocked off other bits of matter at an atomic level by high energy particles from the sun.

The pile of dead humans would sputter and ionise for eons, merging with the substance of the Moon. Maybe they would be the last evidence of humanity once all else had been lost: an organic seep, seventeen kilometres long.

Perhaps aliens, billions of years from now, would ponder the curious abundance of complex organic chemistry in such a narrow strip, imbuing an otherwise grey regolith with oxidised red.

The months passed. At first, it took him nearly two hours to get to the end of the trench, and a further two hours to get back, but that began to diminish as the mountain of bodies became a hill.

Finally, his trench was full. He returned to his garage, and swapped the claw for the last tool he would use – a plough to push the piled up regolith into the trench, covering the bodies.

When he was complete on one side, he drove to the end of the other side of the trench, repeating the process. When he was done, all that was visible was a slightly darkened line where the trench had been. The last, wretched inhabitants of the Pegasus dome had reached their final resting place.

He drove back to his dome for the last time, feeling numb. He was about to be free, about to go back to Earth. Maybe he could find his mother. Maybe move back to London. He doubted it. He suspected that he wasn't going to find Earth welcoming. Perhaps off world would be better: around the moons of Saturn, or further out.

He undressed and washed with gritty water. He

walked, naked, to the comms desk, and pressed some keys. There was a crackle of static.

"I'm finished," he said.

He heard a slight ping, like a small bell being rung. Then explosive charges, laid in a ring around the inside of the dome long before he had moved in, detonated, and he was cast, with an outrush of air, as though from a catapult, far out into the Lunar night.

ABOUT MJ RODDA

MJ Rodda has been writing science fiction short stories since he was at school, and has an embarrassing collection of his stories that were kept by his Mum! He is an avid reader of science fiction and the classics. He recently finished his first novel draft, and hopes to publish it soon.

CHILDREN OF THE SAND

by W. Freedreamer Tinkanesh

Forty kids to escort from Port Central to BioDome One through a sandy desert inhabited by creatures like the giant worm. And what looked like three suns. No wonder it was so hot.

Fortunately, the evenings were cool and the nocturnal cold temperatures bearable. Kids and soldiers wore desert scarves to protect their heads from heatstroke and their noses from the sand carried by the occasional violent gusts of wind. Soldiers wore goggles to protect their eyes. The kids refused the goggles. They had an extra transparent eyelid they could blink into place. Evolution.

The planet's velocity around its three suns was similar to Earth's. We were on the third planet from the Trappist-1 solar system in the Aquarius constellation, thirty-nine light years away from Earth.

The kids kept to themselves most of the time, whispering to each other in a language we didn't understand.

Every evening, Captain Sharid followed the children's lead to establish camp. On the first evening, she ordered a halt. The children's faces were uncertain, and whispers travelled between them. At last, one of them stepped forward and said, "It is not safe here. A desert worm lives under this dune." A finger pointed in the direction of the dune.

Captain Sharid looked at the child thoughtfully for a long while before asking, "Where should we camp then?"

The child looked around, checking their bearings. "This way. Twelve dunes away. It should be safe."

The camp would always be more extended that us soldiers thought was needed. The children asked that we leave them some privacy for the exercise of natural bodily functions. Some of the soldiers laughed, but the Captain stared them down, and granted the children's request.

At night, us soldiers set up our tents in a loose circle at an acceptable distance from them. The children seemed to always find a desert tree to gather around.

On that first evening, a small group of them began busying themselves with something. I approached and saw a scorpion. I pointed my laser gun ready to obliterate the dangerous arachnid, but one of the children put her —or his— hand up.

"No! Let it be! It is not dangerous." The voice was as androgynous as the appearance. They were children of the desert and it was their planet. I guessed they knew better than I did.

The scorpion saw its window of opportunity and ran away. The children laughed and dispersed.

"Okay," I muttered, watching them. They had almost look-a-like appearances: copper-coloured skin from over-exposure to the suns, hair bleached by the harsh light falling short of their shoulders, like everyone we had seen on the planet so far.

The child who had spoken was still standing in front of me, her or his yellow-green eyes studying me. "I'm Keida." The face was serious, the accent as raspy as the sand and as edgy as a rocky mountain.

"I'm Corporal Rayan. You can call me Rayan." I

smiled. But he... she... they... didn't smile back. The children never smiled at the soldiers. We were otherworlders.

We stood there for a minute and the child walked away. Boy or girl? I didn't know. Soldiers speculated about the kids' genders, but no one could figure it out. How old were they? The oldest maybe twelve or thirteen, the youngest five or six.

Every day we walked, the kids as hardy as the soldiers. Their garb was similar to what Tuareg people used to wear in the North-African desert of Earth before it became so hot and so arid that water totally evaporated in every oasis and no caravan could travel across it any more, and even lizards and snakes went sidelining elsewhere.

One evening, I found Private Pike lying on his front at the crest of a dune. He was too intent on his spying, eyes glued to his regulation binoculars, to notice my approach. I grabbed the back of his t-shirt, pulled him roughly and threw him to the sand. Pike was known for his dirty jokes, his dirty mind and his all-around dirty everything.

"Oi!" He rubbed the back of his shaved head. "What's your problem?"

I kicked the erection between his legs.

He screamed, his hands reaching to tenderly cradle the painful body part he was so proud of. He looked at me and grimaced. He suddenly unzipped his trousers and grabbed his swollen penis, showing it off. "Boy or girl, they could all do with some of that!"

I kicked the sand in front of me, hard. The sand flew to his exposed genitals. "Get yourself together, Pike. The Captain wants to see you. Now. And if I see you spying on the kids again, I promise you, you'll regret it with excruciating pain."

Anger distorting his face, he zipped up his trousers and carefully stood up. He picked up his binoculars and walked away, his legs wide apart to favour his painful manhood.

"Rayan."

I turned around. "Keida?"

"Is everything okay?"

"Yes, Keida, everything is okay." I couldn't help but wonder what Pike had seen through his binoculars, if anything at all.

Another child crested the dune. Thinner than Keida, but as tall.

"This is Bat," Keida told me. And to Bat, "This is Rayan. We're safe."

Bat nodded.

I walked back to the main camp. Like every unit, we were only ten soldiers, one corporal, one sergeant, and one captain. While some disliked me, others respected me. Female soldiers knew I'd help them against the likes of Pike if they needed me to. Male soldiers knew to behave in my vicinity. We all wondered about the kids, but they had learned to keep their dirty speculations to themselves in my presence. Except for Pike, of course, who had exasperated even the most patient member of our unit: the captain herself. Pike was famous for having spewed smelly, acidic half-digested rations onto her boots after an evening of heavy drinking. He had spent forty-eight hours in the brig immediately after that. We were then only half-way between Earth and our destination...

Captain Sharid decided that Private Pike had to dig our latrines every evening. He hated it, one shovelling at a time. He hated it even more when he had to bury them in the morning. Some of his fellows had no qualms laughing at the inglorious duty. He blamed me.

*

We stared at the ruins standing in front of us. BioDome One? This was not what we expected: stone walls eroded by the desert winds, a few trees still growing here and there, a broken well where a few lizards sunned themselves. And too small for the city we had imagined.

"Rayan." Captain Sharid turned her hazel eyes to me. "Get one of the kids here. The one who talks to you. Keida, is it?"

"Yes, Captain." I ran to the end of our column, staring at each serious child in turn. Suddenly Keida smiled at me. I also recognized Bat's gloomy expression standing next to... them. "Keida. Captain Sharid asked to see you."

"Of course. She wants to know where we're at."

We walked back at a brisk pace. When we reached the Captain, I could see fascination in Keida's eyes.

"What is this place? Is it BioDome One?" The Captain was frowning.

"No, it is Klibah, the Forgotten City. It was abandoned a long time ago. It was beautiful. I've seen pictures."

"What kind of people lived here?"

Keida shrugged their shoulders. "People." Their eyes scanned the landscape all around us. "We should camp here tonight. On this side of Klibah. There are desert worms on the other side."

Captain Sharid watched Keida walk off, then looked at me and sighed, "Kids... Okay. It's early, but never mind. We don't want to deal with these bloody worms more than necessary." Her eyes searched for someone and zeroed in on him. She hollered, "Sergeant McCloud!"

A skinny man with broad shoulders ran up and smartly saluted. "Captain!"

Some of the kids were already checking out the tree and exploring some of the ruins. I noticed Pike walking to the broken well and swiftly grabbing one of the lizards by its tail. A small child approached and spoke to him. The tone was serious, the words in their language. Pike laughed his malevolent laugh. I joined them and noticed the lust in Pike's eyes.

"What's going on?"

The child simply pointed a finger at the lizard.

"What?" said Pike. "Lizard meat would be a change from the rations."

"For all you know, it could be poisonous."

He stopped smiling. "Spoilsport." He dropped the lizard and walked off, kicking sand with his boots.

The lizard ran off to find its friends. The child nodded to me, apparently satisfied, and ran off to find the other kids. Children of the sand and protectors of lizards? Or had they saved Pike's life? They were a mystery.

Us, Earthlings – new to the planet – had been asked to escort the children as a sign of good will and willingness towards a peaceful and respectful relationship with the natives. The commander in charge of our incursion to Trappist-1 had agreed.

There had been a nomadic people taking these children across the desert, but they had disappeared and now the kids were overdue north-east. Or so we had been told. It was something of an enigma. While the natives we had met seemed to have a primitive technology, they were highly cultured, and while we struggled with the grammatical structure of their language, they had no problems learning military English. Apparently, they had at least two dozen words for sand and twice more for wind. They were peaceful people, but there was a predatory hint in their eyes. The adults appeared different to the children. All the adults, even though without facial hair, seemed male. Where were the women? I don't think anyone got an answer, because the word would have spread like wild fire...

But back to the desert. Sand covered only a quarter of the planet, and water about half. The last quarter was green plains and green mountains, but we had only detected signs of human life in the desert. Electronic interference got in the way of our scanning in the forests.

I was a soldier by choice. Not much else to do on the overcrowded planet Earth had become. When I heard about the first manned mission to Trappist-1, I volunteered. I had no family. I wasn't afraid of a few months in a cramped military spaceship. Some didn't survive. Some were still recovering. It was a wonder that Pike, as unbalanced as he was, seemed to do so well. I don't think anyone would have missed him. Except for his mother.

The walls of Kiblah were darker than the traditional ochre structures at Port Central. The temperature during the day was still a record high. The kids didn't seem to mind. The night temperature was slightly cooler.

That evening, while a group of us were quietly staring at the camp fire after eating our rations, a sound jerked us back to reality.

The children were singing: the sweet voices of girls, or boys before puberty. It was haunting, spellbinding. We stared at each other in amazement. Even Pike's face softened. It was the first time we had heard them singing. Was it a special rite or a ceremony for the forgotten city of Klibah?

That night, I dreamed the people of Klibah were

hardy, wiry, and as tall as Masai.

But I still couldn't figure out their gender. I was secretly as curious as every soldier. Was there such a notion as gender on the third planet of Trappist-1? They were used to our physical differences now, but at first their puzzlement had been obvious. It was not just that they got used to us, it was more a case of carelessly discarding the subject. It seemed to have no value and no interest for them. Strange people. We could barely comprehend their culture. They seem so peaceful, despite the predatory glare in the eyes of the adults at Port Central. And the children... they didn't seem to belong with them. Was it why we were asked to take them to BioDome One? Their skin tone was lighter, their features less sharp. Captain Sharid had a degree in anthropology, but she was careful to keep her observations and speculations to herself, and for the report she'd write later.

*

BioDome One was made of yellow and red ochre with a geodesic structure that shone in the midst of traditional houses. A trumpet sounded from the closest minaret: a long, clear sound aimed at the sky.

Soon, a person wearing a white djellabah and a pale blue headscarf walked towards us. Captain Sharid greeted the dignitary.

First, they bowed at each other, keeping eye contact, as we had learned was their tradition. Keida ran to them and bowed their head, too. The dignitary spoke a long sentence with a chaotic accent. I think the first word meant 'welcome' and somewhere in the mix another word meant 'expected'. Another word might have been 'storm'.

Keida translated, "Welcome, people of the faraway sister planet. You have been expected. You arrive at a most extreme time to take shelter, as a storm is brewing in the north."

We looked to the north. The sky was a blue hardened by solar heat. Not a hint of cloud.

The dignitary smiled, their features as soft as the children's, and their eyes, full of curiosity, and as green as the forests we were not allowed to visit. They spoke again.

Keida translated again, "The skies of BioDome One are always deceptive, but the air tells us everything we need to know. Please," the left arm extended towards the city. "Come and take shelter. We have quarters ready for you. And the children," their smile widened, "are a wonder to lay eyes upon." Keida smiled.

Our caravan followed the dignitary in their footsteps. Sand started to dance in the air currents here and there as we reached the first houses. The streets were empty. I guessed the people were all in their houses. Windows were shuttered with planks of wood. Wood? Where were they getting wood from?

The dignitary picked up their pace on the main street towards the geodesic dome. Its windows, too, were barred with wood. We followed our guide, taking a sharp left into a tall earth structure just before the street circling the central dome. We found ourselves in a wide room with wide steps carved in the rocky ground, leading deep underground. Two people waited at the foot of the stairs with torches that gave off an aroma of sweet oil and incense. The first sharp crack of thunder sounded as we entered a tunnel.

At the end, we entered a wide, round and natural room washed in wavering light from torches hung on the walls.

It was completely empty. The dignitary gestured towards one of many openings: one with no shadow fluttering over its threshold.

Keida, Bat, and the other kids rushed for it, laughing and chatting. Keida stopped suddenly, walked back towards me and declared, "We will see you later. I'll be your mediator." She flashed me a happy smile and ran after the other kids.

Mediator? The dignitary gestured towards another light-bathed opening. We slowly and cautiously crossed the threshold into a bare room, empty except for a natural pond in one corner: our guest quarters.

Like almost every other soldier there, my heart rose at the thought of finally being able to wash the dust and sweat from my skin. Almost every other soldier. Out of the corner of my eye, I caught Pike's mouth turn up in a smirk.

But before I could rebuke him, one of the female soldiers turned towards him. "One lustful look from you and I won't just erase it from your face, I will kill you with my bare hands."

Pike smirked and shrugged his shoulders as a reply.

"Quiet!" Captain Sharid said. "I expect each of you to behave. We all need a wash. We'll take turns."

*

While the people of the third planet from the Trappist-1 system were willing to welcome newcomers, they were also cautious. I didn't blame them. Earth history was riddled with too much greed even if they knew nothing about it.

During our stay at BioDome One, we were not invited into the geodesic structure, I suspected due to technology that they weren't prepared to share with us. How else could they communicate with Port Central and other cities around the planet? But they didn't seem to care much for it. They were peaceful people. Quick learners, too, like the people of Port Central. And as much of a mystery.

As a mediator, Keida was present for every dealing with the dignitary. Keida was more than a mere translator, they would describe cultural differences in both languages. A facilitator, a communicator, a guide. I was impressed by their intelligence. Because they took me to many corners of the city, I got to witness many of their cultural quirkiness. As a consequence, I had many conversations with Captain Sharid to complement her anthropological report.

Still, the question remained. Were they intersex, or simply non-binary? Pike had no luck with any of the androgynous people he tried to have conversations with. Mostly, they just laughed at him.

The dignitary asked us to take another group of children with us for our return trip to Port Central.

They were different from Keida's group, and different again from the adults of BioDome One. They reminded us of the people at Port Central. What was the exchange about? Gifts to insure peace? They seemed to know nothing of war and its consequences.

When the Captain asked, the dignitary explained. "It has always been so. Our children flourish better with the climate of Port Central, and the children of Port Central flourish better in the climate here." Or something else they wouldn't share with us, despite Captain Sharid's subtle queries.

*

We left BioDome One with as many questions as we had arrived with, and with a group of forty-two children who never smiled.

I wore a pendant under my desert gear that had been made and gifted to me by Keida to remember them. It was a small, red semi-precious stone shaped like a lizard.

The trip back was uneventful, except for Private Pike falling foul of a desert worm under the feral eyes of forty-two quiet children. Since he didn't have any mother, no one missed him.

ABOUT W.FREEDREAMER TINKANESH

W. Freedreamer Tinkanesh is a dreamer, a tree hugger, a musician, an animal lover, an artist, a private person, a speculative writer and much more. W has published a vampire novel ('Outsider') and a collection of diverse short stories ('Tales for the 21st Century'). While mostly dark fantasy, W's work has been featured in anthologies of horror and fantasy. W has no gender and their preferred pronoun is 'they'.

Goodreads: https://www.goodreads.com/author/show/5834080.W_Freedreamer_Tinkanesh
LiveJournal: http://lordwalkiwolf.livejournal.com/
Twitter: https://twitter.com/LordWalkiWolf
Facebook: https://www.facebook.com/Walkis-Monster-156907977708751/

EDITOR'S NOTE

Thank you for reading *Another Place*. We hope you enjoyed it.

If you're a fan of poetry or flash fiction and would like to contribute to the charity and get another great read into the bargain, you might be interested in *Voices along the Road*, a collection of refugee-themed poetry and flash fiction.

Like *Another Place*, all profits are donated to the Alf Dubs Children's Fund.

If you'd like to find out more about the great work that the Alf Dubs Children's Fund does, visit:

http://safepassage.org.uk/what-we-do/alf-dubs-fund/

Printed in Great Britain
by Amazon